"Wel   **art.
Tell**   **ned
back in his chair and slanted his eyes
toward her.**

As he took her in, he realized his chocolate beauty
was probably thanking heaven her beautiful,
delicious dark skin wouldn't show any signs of
blushing.

She looked really cute when she was contrite, and he
found himself enjoying her uneasy stance.

"I'm sorry. I don't usually give my opinion in this
manner with clients. You can of course feel any way
you wish. I just wanted to highlight that you really
have a lot to be thankful for…" Her voice trailed off.

"Oh, your point is very much noted, *Ms.* Dash."

He watched her back straighten and her hand
absently twirl her hair. She sucked her bottom lip
in and nibbled on it for a moment, and in that
moment he wished he were her teeth.

He wanted to nibble and suck on those lips in the
worst way.

Clarity struck. In that very moment, he realized no
matter what he was going to have to kiss Little Miss
Spitfire soon.

Books by Gwyneth Bolton

Kimani Romance

Protect and Serve
Make It Hot

GWYNETH BOLTON

was born and raised in Paterson, New Jersey. She currently lives in central New York with her husband, Cedric. When she was twelve years old, she became an avid reader of romance by sneaking her mother's stash of Harlequin and Silhouette novels. In the nineties, she was introduced to African-American and multicultural romance novels, and her life hasn't been the same since. She has a B.A. and M.A. in English/creative writing and a Ph.D. in English/composition and rhetoric. She teaches classes on writing and women's studies at the college level. She has won several awards for her romance novels, including four Emma Awards and a Romance in Color Reviewers' Choice Award for New Author of the Year. When she is not teaching or working on her own romance novels, she is curled up with a cup of herbal tea, a warm quilt and a good book. She can be reached via e-mail at gwynethbolton@prodigy.net, and readers can visit her Web site at www.gwynethbolton.com.

Make it
HOT

Gwyneth Bolton

KIMANI
ROMANCE

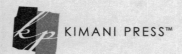 KIMANI PRESS™

ISBN-13: 978-0-373-86083-8
ISBN-10:   0-373-86083-8

MAKE IT HOT

www.kimanipress.com

Printed in U.S.A.

Dear Reader,

Thanks for taking the time to read Joel and Samantha's story. Every now and then a couple comes to my imagination and they are so perfect for each other they *almost* lull me into believing that telling their story will be a snap. Joel and Samantha were two peas in a pod, but writing their story was *not* easy.

These two characters proved to me without a doubt that even when the loving is easy, staying together and building something worth having is difficult—but worthwhile—work. What would you do if loving someone meant you might lose your job? What would you do if the career that you'd had for a long time, that made up such a large part of your identity, was no longer an option for you? Would you be able to open yourself to love no matter how vulnerable it made you feel? Joel and Samantha took a chance and opened up their hearts and souls to love. I hope their story inspires you to take a chance, too.

Be sure to pick up my December 2008 release, *The Law of Desire,* for the next installment in the HIGHTOWER HONORS series: four brothers on a mission to protect, serve and love…

Gwyneth Bolton

First I want to thank God for the many blessings in my life, especially the blessing to share my stories. I'd like to thank my family: my mother, Donna, my sisters Jennifer, Cassandra, Michelle and Tashina, my nieces Ashlee and Zaria and my husband Cedric. And I'd like to thank all the readers who have taken the time to write me and let me know what they thought of my novels. Your words have meant more than you could ever know.

To my readers, thank you for reading the words I write and inspiring me to write the best books I possibly can.

Prologue

"He's gotta be okay, man. This is Joel we're talking about!" A raspy voice choked out the words as two emergency medical technicians wheeled a stretcher past Samantha Dash, almost knocking her out of the way.

"Excuse us, miss. We need to get through here." The taller of the two technicians pulling up the rear was at least courteous as he brushed past her.

Samantha nodded and stepped out of the way as two firefighters dressed in full gear with faces full of soot and grime followed the EMTs. The patient was clearly one of their own.

The firefighters were led back out to the waiting room by the head nurse. Instead of heading back to the clinic next door where she worked, Samantha decided to stick around for a minute.

She had been in the emergency room, showing a patient with a broken leg how to use crutches. Normally, she never paid any attention to the hustle and bustle of the E.R. when she was called in from the clinic to do crutch care. Most physical therapists found it to be the most tedious part of the job, but they knew the small service meant a lot to patients getting used to walking with crutches. Somebody had to show them how to use the things; plus, this time she'd picked the shortest straw so out of the few physical therapists, it was her turn.

"What happened?" Samantha asked the head nurse. Nurse Madison was all of five feet tall but ran the E.R. like a drill sergeant. She also knew more about what was going on in the hospital than anyone on staff.

"I just had to show those two where they could wait. Things are going to get crazy hectic around here in a minute. That big warehouse fire downtown got out of control, and at least one firefighter was badly injured. Before you know it, this place is going to be swarming with firemen, media folk…and if this guy is who I heard them say he was, we've got a whole heap of Hightowers on the way." Nurse Madison placed her pointer finger on her chin before turning to another nurse who happened to be walking by. "Is that Joel Hightower back there? One of Sophie's nephews?"

The red-haired and freckled nurse stopped and nodded. "Yep, and you know 'Ms. Retired' will be here trying to tell us all what to do in a bit."

"Mmm, hmm. That's what I thought. Lord Jesus, I don't need this. I ain't able to deal with that woman today." Nurse Madison spun and took off down the hall, full of sprite for an older woman. She turned and waved. "Gotta go, sweetie."

Samantha didn't have any more appointments at the clinic, so she followed Nurse Madison and watched as the doctors ran to and fro working on the firefighter.

"He'll be lucky to walk again. Both legs are broken—the tibia and fibula on the right and the tibia on the left, and the injuries to the back and spine are extensive." Dr. Lardner, a blond, old world, Viking-looking man, noted with a frown.

"The cervical, thoracic and lumbar regions of the spine are severely damaged. We have to operate if he is going to have a shot at walking again, much less fight fires," Dr. Samuels, an older fair-skinned African-American concluded.

Samantha winced as she listened to the doctors. As

a physical therapist, she knew enough about back injuries to know it didn't look good for the man. And back surgery had the fifty-fifty chance of making things better or worse.

"A damn shame, too. He's so young..." Nurse Madison *tsked* as they rushed the patient out of the E.R.

"Let's roll, people. Let's get him prepped and ready for the O.R...." The bass in the doctor's voice more than hinted at the urgency.

The doctors and nurses rolled the patient away, and Samantha walked back toward the waiting room. More firefighters had shown up, just like Nurse Madison had predicted. They were all pacing the room as they waited to hear about their colleague.

Several more people came bursting through the automatic door and into the waiting room. They all had on formal wear and went right toward the firemen. The men were in tuxedos, and some of the younger women were dressed in matching red satin gowns. The family looked as if they had been at a wedding or something.

Nurse Madison walked out and spoke to them. Many of the women buried their heads in the men's chests and cried. The men had stunned expressions, and they looked as if they wanted to sob. Watching them hold each other and support one another,

Samantha found it hard to leave and return to the clinic. She couldn't seem to pull her gaze away, and she couldn't stop thinking about the firefighter they were all pulling for. The energy in the room felt electric, and the family was doing exactly what they were *supposed* to be doing at a time like this. They were there for each other to lean on. She knew first-hand that didn't always happen.

A searing pain laced up Joel Hightower's spine and cut clear through to his soul. He could hear faint crying in the background.

Is that my mother? What is she doing crying?

He tried to open his mouth, but even the slightest movement caused the pain to slice him even more.

What in the hell happened to me?

He could vaguely remember fire. There had been flames all around him, and heat... Such intense heat... He remembered falling. The floor must have given way.

Oh, God.

Now, the pain in his spine took on new meaning, and he almost cried out.

What if the pain signaled something larger?

What if he could never walk again?

Never put out another fire?

They might as well kill me now.

He heard it again. Delicate sniffles and a soft voice. He was sure it was his mother. He felt her hand on him, and he heard more crying, familiar voices.

Men. His brothers. His father.

Joel Hightower tried to open his eyes, but the drowsiness overcame him like a dark cloak numbing his senses and dulling his brain. Tired and overwhelmed, he could no longer fight.

Samantha flipped through the channels, stopping at the news coverage of the warehouse fire. The images were horrific. Thankfully there hadn't been any fatalities. Yet.

"Tragedy has befallen one of North Jersey's most beloved families of public servants, the Hightowers. This family, with its legacy of firefighters and police officers, is waiting to see if one of their own will walk again after a horrendous accident. Thirty-five-year-old Joel Hightower, a Paterson, New Jersey, fireman, was gravely injured fighting a fire in an abandoned warehouse in downtown Paterson today. The well-liked young man joined the fire department right out of college and has been a fireman for thirteen years. Hightower fell nine stories down through a burning floor, and doctors are speculating on whether this young hero will walk again."

The young newswoman's upbeat tone seemed to

be in direct contrast to the news she reported. As she spoke, a picture of Joel flashed on the screen.

He was casually dressed in the picture. He had big brown eyes with a slightly mischievous gleam. Remembering his supportive, large family and looking at his frozen smile now, Samantha felt as if she could glimpse a piece of his soul. She gazed at his deep chocolate pools. She bet his somewhat devilish smile constantly kept folks guessing. She couldn't tell for sure if he was a serious guy or a practical joker, but she would have put money on practical joker.

His strong jawline and features were softened by the hint of playfulness that seemed to exude from him. Then, all too soon, the picture she'd been studying moved from the screen, and the perky blond newswoman was back.

Nothing like being jerked right back to reality.

"Like many members of the Hightower family, including the chief of the Paterson police department, Kendall Hightower, Joel is very active in the community, coaching Little League and being a member of the Big Brother program."

The screen showed footage of what appeared to be a Little League baseball team winning a game. Seeing Joel jumping up and down in a celebratory manner with the little boys made her heart swell. The young boys looked almost as happy as Joel did. *Exuberant* was not too strong a word to encompass the person who seemed to leap from the screen. The community couldn't afford to lose a man who did so much good with the youth.

She *really* hoped he pulled through.

The news program switched to footage of him and a bunch of men playing basketball. Samantha moved a little closer to the screen and saw the team in red—his team—wore shirts that read "*Hightower Firemen.*" The other team had on shirts that read "*Hightower Cops.*" The firemen had apparently won the game because Joel was jumping up and down and laughing.

She smiled at the sound of his hearty laughter.

"Our street reporter, Kasey West, was able to talk with some of his coworkers and the doctors treating him at St Joseph's Medical Center."

Samantha watched man after man become choked up as they tried to talk about their colleague and friend. She knew he had to be a really great guy to inspire that kind of raw emotion in those big, strapping firemen. They all had positive things to say about him. Phrases like *all-around good guy, brave beyond compare, loads of fun,* and *involved citizen,* were expressed more than a few times. She was glad the reporter had enough decency not to bother the family members.

Turning off the television, she went to sleep with

Joel Hightower firmly on her mind. His smiling face and laughter filled her dreams.

The next morning, she picked up her paper only to find him on the front page. He was wearing his formal fireman uniform. Judging by the glowing story written about him, he appeared to be the picture of bravery. She had to make herself put the newspaper down and finish her coffee so she could make it to work on time.

What is the deal with me? I can't believe I'm thinking about him this much....

She had to stop in the hospital on a consult for another patient, and she went by the firefighter's room just to make sure he was doing all right. While she certainly couldn't take anything away from him or men like him, she felt bad for the women they left behind. Women like her mother. Women like the injured fireman's poor mother who sat there crying her eyes out and begging God to make her son well, to let her son live and be able to walk again.

Samantha had seen enough of that growing up, and she couldn't see herself being with a man in a dangerous job and ending up in the same predicament. Once was enough.

She was about to walk back out of the room when the older woman looked up. The medium-built woman was dressed in a stylish eggplant colored pantsuit with a string of pearls and matching earrings. Her salt-and-pepper hair was up in a bun and her smooth brown complexion was flawless. Minus the gray hair, she hardly seemed old enough to have an adult child.

"Are you another one of the doctors?" The woman wiped the tears from her eyes but more replaced them.

"No, ma'am. I'm a physical therapist. I saw his story on the news and just wanted to stop by and share some positive energy and thoughts." Samantha smiled and started to leave the room again. She felt awkward being there, since she didn't even know the man.

"He has to pull through. I can't lose my child." His mother buried her head in her arms and started sobbing.

Samantha walked over to the woman and placed her arms around her.

"He'll make it." As she said the words of comfort, she realized how true she wanted them to be. It would be a shame for this woman to lose her son, for the world to lose such a brave man.

"Out of all my boys, he was always the prankster, guaranteed to go out of his way to bring a smile to my face." She lifted her head, and it seemed as if she was trying to smile as she remembered her son's antics; but the smile was shaky at best.

"If he weren't the one laid up there like that, he'd

be in here with me now saying or doing something to try and stop me from crying."

So, I was right about him.

Samantha prided herself on being a good judge of people, and it pleased her to know that she had read Joel Hightower's kind, handsome face correctly. He was a joker. He would probably make her laugh all the time.

She shook her head.

Where in the hell did that thought come from?

Samantha gazed at the sleeping man, but looking at his striking brown face, which seemed somewhere between restful and tense, she could tell the first operation must have been excruciating. She had overheard the doctors saying they needed to do at least one more operation on his spine.

"He'll be fine, and he'll make you laugh again, Mrs. Hightower." Samantha offered the only words of encouragement she could. She knew the man had a long road to travel toward recovery, but looking at him, she also knew he'd make it.

She prayed he would.

She and Mrs. Hightower sat in silence. The only sound heard was Joel's mother's soft sobs. The only thing Samantha could think was she never wanted to be the woman crying because she'd been foolish enough to fall for a man who had a dangerous job.

She would *never* make that mistake.

* * *

"So what exactly are you saying to me, Doc? Make it plain."

Joel listened to everything the man was saying, and he didn't like any of it. After two painful surgeries and spending more time than he could have ever wanted laid up in a hospital bed in traction, he had very little patience for medical jargon and even less patience for hypothetical ponderings.

He wanted to know one thing and one thing only: Would he be able to fight fires again?

The distinguished surgeon, Dr. Lardner, gave an uncharacteristically sheepish grin that seemed to acknowledge he'd been guilty of not being as clear or as forthcoming as he could have been. His thin lips pursed in consideration, and his thick blond eyebrows closed in at the middle of his forehead. He ran his hand through perfectly coiffed blond hair, then stared at Joel with steel-blue eyes.

"Your surgeries were very successful, and the extent of the damage to your spine was not as extensive as we had originally thought. We honestly didn't think you would walk again. We thought you would have been at the very least partially paralyzed—at the worst, fully paralyzed—but you're not." Dr. Lardner stopped and gave Joel a pointed look before continuing.

"You will be able to walk once your legs and spine

heal, but you will need intense physical therapy to strengthen the spine and to help get you to the point where you are walking with the same proficiency you were before the accident. Is that *plain* enough for you?"

Joel bit back the sarcastic quip he was thinking as the doctor threw his own words back at him. He wasn't used to feeling so on edge and vulnerable. However, not being able to get around and move the way he wanted to was taking its toll, and the thought that he might not be able to do the one thing he had wanted to do ever since he was a little boy—fight fires—had him feeling more like a tiger in a cage than a guy in traction.

"Yeah, I get it, Doc. I'm lucky I'll be able to walk again, but will I be able to fight fires again?" Joel gritted his teeth to hold back the rest of what he wanted to say. No need pissing off the skillful surgeon whose hands made walking again a reality.

"That I can't tell you, Joel." Dr. Lardner gave a slight shrug. "Once you're out of here and have started and completed your physical therapy, we'll have a better sense of that. But for now, let's dwell on getting you healed up so that you can go out there and handle the rest. Okay?"

Joel nodded. He would go back to his profession because any alternative to that was *not* an option. Fighting fires were not only his legacy, but also his entire reason for being.

Going one-on-one, head-to-head against one of nature's most destructive elements was the biggest rush he'd ever felt. He fought fires because he loved helping people. He fought fires because he was a part of an elite group of men who lived to do what no one else would: run into the blaze not away from it. He didn't have the kind of personality that would allow him to just sit behind a desk day after day. He needed to be out and in the thick of things.

Taming a fire before it spread and took lives or wrestling a life out of the fire's hands by carrying a child or adult to safety from a burning building made him feel as if he could *really* do anything he wanted. To say his profession was intimately connected to his sense of manhood would have been an *enormous* understatement, and that was why he had to be able to fight fires again. That was why he *would* be able to fight them again. He couldn't let anyone or anything stand in his way.

Chapter 1

Six months later

Joel Hightower entered the physical-therapy stage of his rehabilitation feeling less like his normal upbeat self.

Okay, make that nothing like his normal self.

After the two operations on his back, he had spent the bulk of the past five months in traction, and once the casts had come off, he'd had to get used to walking around with a cane for a little while, walking around feeling like half the man he used to be.

As far as he was concerned, he was allowed to be

in a bad mood. His entire life had been snatched from under him, and he had to literally learn how to walk on his own two feet again.

The inside of the clinic looked as drab as the adjacent hospital had. Sure, the walls of the waiting room were a bright shade of Pepto pink, but everything else screamed stale and antiseptic. He really hoped the rest of the clinic wasn't the same color scheme. He couldn't take three months of constant puke pink.

He had to get his body back functioning properly so he could get a clean bill of health to return to his job. That was the most important thing. Getting back to work. Putting out fires. Until then, he felt as if he was on hold.

Too bad his physical therapist was keeping him waiting, too. He stood, freed himself from his brother Lawrence's helpful grasp and steadied himself on his cane as he walked over to the receptionist's desk for the second time in twenty minutes.

The short, perky woman had her shoulder-length hair pulled back in a ponytail and wore very little makeup on her almond-colored face. He glanced at the nameplate on her desk. Jenny Saunders.

"Ms. Saunders, I—" he started, only to be cut off with a honey-sweet smile.

"She's running a little behind. This isn't normally the case. She'll be right with you. Again, I apologize for the delay. We had a therapist call in sick today, and Samantha had to take on some of his patients."

The woman gave him another pleasant grin and a stare that seemed to suggest he go and sit down somewhere. He could tell Jenny Saunders was getting a little tired of him.

So what? He was tired of waiting.

His therapist's first-impression points were going down—way down.

"Why don't you just chill, man? Have a seat. Relax." His brother Lawrence was only a couple of years older than him. The way the narcotics detective was always telling Joel what to do, one would think Lawrence had him by decades.

Although all the Hightower men shared the same mahogany complexions, dashing good looks and athletic builds, he and Lawrence had often been mistaken for twins when they were growing up. He used to hate that.

He decided to ignore Lawrence for the moment.

"It's not like you walking up there every five minutes is going to make your therapist come any faster," Lawrence offered.

When he realized Joel was not going to respond, Lawrence shrugged and went back to flipping through the *Vibe* magazine he'd gotten from the humongous pile of reading materials on the coffee table.

"I'm sorry I'm late. I'm Samantha Dash, and you must be Mr. Hightower."

He turned to set eyes on a curvy chocolate goddess with flashing brown eyes, flawlessly smooth skin and jet-black hair. She wore her hair in one of those natural styles with twists, and it reached her shoulders. Then there was her smile… With a smile like hers she could probably get away with anything.

Anything but keep him waiting.

Forget how captivating she looked. "Do you always disregard your patients' time like this, or is it just me? Because if this is the way you conduct yourself, then maybe I should look into getting another therapist."

She tilted her head, and she took a step back, placing her hand on her hip. She glared at him for a full minute before saying a word.

Joel glanced at Lawrence for some moral support and saw his brother had buried his face in the magazine.

No problem. He didn't need backup for this. Right was right and wrong was wrong.

"Like I said, I apologize. We're down one therapist today, but that's not your problem. The gift of understanding isn't something everyone is born with. *So,* I'm sorry for giving you the opportunity to exhibit your extreme lack in that area. Now, if you'll just follow me, we can get you started." Her smile took on a decidedly false appearance, and gone was the warmth and kindness that seemed to exude from her just a few moments ago.

Oh, well.

That wasn't his problem. He was there for one reason and one reason only, to get his life back, and if this hand-on-hip, smart-mouth spitfire of a woman had to be checked from the door in order to ensure he got what he needed, then so be it.

Well, pictures certainly are deceiving. Samantha led Joel Hightower back into her office in the clinic. She had been a little nervous when she found out she was the therapist assigned to the hero firefighter. The fact that she had thought of him often over the past six months made her think she might be risking her usual professional distance with him as a patient.

Meeting the incorrigible, surly man in person let her know right away she had *nothing* to worry about. She didn't have to worry about being attracted to him. Hell, she didn't have to worry about even liking this man. He was nothing like the playful, mischievously sexy stud she had conjured up in her imagination.

That guy would probably always have a funny joke and a smile. That guy had sex appeal for days and would make a woman run hot, not with anger the way she was at the moment, but with passion.

That guy didn't exist and in his place was *this* jerk.

"First off, I'd like to tell you a little bit about what you'll be doing here for the next three months." She kept her tone even and flat as they sat in her office.

It was a small office with an even tinier window, but it was hers. At twenty-seven years old, she liked the fact she had worked hard and secured a position with excellent growth opportunities at such a high-profile clinic attached to a renowned hospital and medical center.

One day she would have a bigger office and even more patients, but for now, she made this one cozy with lots of earth tones and faux plants. She would have loved real plants, but her first efforts of using real greenery to beautify her space ended in carnage. It would have rivaled the destruction of the rain forests if she hadn't performed a self-intervention and embraced her lack of a green thumb.

During her first time meeting with a patient, she liked to give them a sense of what to expect. So she talked with them in her office for about twenty to thirty minutes depending on her first impression of the patient's personality and the injuries each had sustained. At the end of each session, she spoke with them to wrap things up.

"My job is to help improve the function and mobility in your back. To help you begin to walk more fluidly. I'm also here to help relieve the pain and teach you exercise and pain-management techniques. We'll run some general exercises today, testing your strength, balance, coordination, posture and muscle performance."

He sighed and rolled his eyes.

Oh. No. He. Didn't.

"I'm sorry, Mr. Hightower, but am I boring you? Does the discussion of how I plan to help you with your back bother you?" She knew her tone was snappy, but she couldn't help it.

He sighed again. "I heard all of this from my doctor. I know what a physical therapist is supposed to do, so can we get to it and just do it?"

Oh. Yes. He. Did.

How could she have been so wrong about a person? This impatient, irritable man was nothing like she had imagined, nothing like the man she had dreamed of him being. She almost wished she had never met him. At least then she would still have her sweet version of him to think about.

She plastered on her most professional smile. "Fine. I can explain as we go along."

You surly sourpuss of a man!

Once she started working with him, things went somewhat smoothly. As long as they didn't try to have a conversation, they were fine.

After working with him on balance, coordination and trying to get him used to moving around without the cane, she decided to try another shot at small talk. They had three months of therapy to get through, after all. It would be nice if they could build at least a cordial working relationship.

Basketball!

What man didn't like to talk about sports? And the Nets and the Knicks were both having great seasons. As a Jersey guy, he was bound to be a fan of one of those teams.

Being a Chi-town girl, she personally liked the Bulls over *all* teams. She had been a fan since the days of Michael Jordan and she believed he was the greatest player to have ever played the game.

No one compared. *No* one.

And she included the Bulls in her prayers at least once a week—two or three times during the play-offs— in hopes the team would return to its former glory.

But she could squelch her fandom to reach out to a patient. She didn't *hate* the Nets or the Knicks. She could tolerate those teams and their fans. As long as he wasn't a Lakers fan or God forbid a Phoenix Suns fan, they could have a nice conversation.

"So, what do you think about the Nets?"

He shrugged. "I don't think about them. I'm not really a fan of the team."

"Oh, so you're a Knicks fan?"

"Knicks? No way. That's my brother Lawrence's favorite team. I can't stand them. They invent new ways to lose a game. Sorriest team in the league, well minus the Chicago Bulls, who haven't seen a good year since that highly overrated ball hog Jordan left." He laughed.

The hair stood up on the back of her neck and her lip twisted to the side.

Did he just call Jordan overrated and the Bulls sorry?

Her mind did a rewind as she replayed his blasphemous words in her mind. Sure, she'd wanted him to lighten up so they could connect, but...

"Actually, I'm a former Lakers fan. Now it's all about the Suns. Shaq Diesel will go down in history as the best to ever play the game." He flexed an arm muscle and nodded.

She could only assume he was trying to convince himself that the nonsense he was spouting was somehow true.

"On what planet? You must be delusional. Even if Michael Jordan had never played the game, Shaq would hardly qualify as the best to ever play it. And really...the Lakers? The Suns? That just lets me know you don't have a thing to say about the sport worth listening to." As soon as the words came out of her mouth, she winced.

She turned and looked at him and saw he was staring at her with a perplexed expression.

"So, because I like a different team and don't think
Jordan hung the moon, then I just need to shut up?"

*Well, when you say it like that, it does sound
kind of harsh.*

She took a deep breath.

It was on the tip of her tongue to tell Mr. Hightower, "yes, shut up!" He made her mouth go on
extra-overload saying things she would have never
said to a patient, ever.

Her father used to take her to see the Bulls when she
was a kid. After he was gone, she still watched all the
games on television when she could. It had been the
one thing she could do to remain close to him.

However, she could *maybe, possibly,* put her feelings on hold for a minute.

"No, of course you don't need to shut up. You can
certainly voice your opinions, no matter how woefully
misguided they are."

*Now, see, you could have left off the woefully mis-
guided part, Samantha,* she told herself.

"How about we just leave basketball alone?"

"That's probably a good idea." She used her fake
but very professional smile again. "So, I want to try
a little electric stimulation today. It's one of the meth-
ods we use to relieve pain."

It was better to just stick to the basics with this guy. The only thing they seemed to have in common was getting him well.

Chapter 2

Driving back to his town house in Passaic Park with his brother, Joel couldn't stop talking about his physical therapist. She was certainly great at what she did. In one session, she had put him through more activity than he'd seen in months, and it seemed like the more irritated she became with him, the more she did.

He had a feeling Lawrence was a little bit tired of him talking about Samantha Dash, but every time he thought he was done, he would remember something else.

By the time they were sitting in his living room watching a basketball game on his large flat-screen television, he remembered the horrified look on her face when he had made his comment about Michael Jordan. You would have thought he'd said the Easter Bunny and Santa Claus should be executed at the firing range.

She rebounded quickly though. Yes, Samantha Dash seemed to be quite the trouper. He smiled.

"What are you grinning about now?" Lawrence studied him a little too intently before shrugging. "You got anything to eat in this place? How're we supposed to watch the game with no snacks?"

"There's some stuff back there. You know Mama and Aunt Sophie have been trying to outdo one another by keeping my fridge and my cupboards full."

Lawrence's eyes lit up. Although all of his brothers loved their mother's cooking, Lawrence swore by it. In fact, he vowed he wouldn't marry a woman if she couldn't come close to his mother's cuisine. Since they didn't make them like Celia Hightower anymore, Joel figured the proclamation was Lawrence's slick way of remaining a bachelor forever.

"Okay, what did Aunt Sophie make and what did Mama make?" Lawrence called back as he darted into the kitchen.

"I'm not sure. You'll have to taste and see."

"Aww, man! You know Aunt Sophie can't cook. You're supposed to make note of stuff like that.

Why're you keeping her food anyway? You're supposed to throw that stuff right out in the trash. I swear, some of her food is toxic," Lawrence yelled from the kitchen.

Joel laughed as he heard Lawrence gag and curse. He must have sampled one of Aunt Sophie's masterpieces.

By the time Lawrence came back with his plate of "safe" Mama-made food, Joel thought he'd finally finished thinking about his physical therapist.

Then he thought about the sparks that flew out of her eyes when he snapped at her about being late. For a moment she'd looked at him as if she wanted to rake him over the coals. She was a full of fire for sure.

Little Miss Spitfire. That's what she was.

He smiled again.

"What do you keep smiling about?" Lawrence asked as he placed his plate on the dark oak end table and leaned back in the deep burgundy leather recliner he always sat in when he came by.

Normally, Joel preferred the recliner for himself, but in the spirit of being a good host, he always allowed Lawrence to sit there. Ever since they'd been kids, Lawrence had pretty much ignored boundaries. If you let on something was your favorite, he took it over.

Favorite cup, ink pen, hat, whatever. Once Lawrence found out, you'd find him using it. He liked to irritate folks. It was easier to ignore him, but Joel was the only brother who could really do it. Both Patrick and Jason pitched fits when they found Lawrence using their favorite cup or pen. Joel let it slide. So, he made the matching leather sofa his spot whenever Lawrence was around.

"I was just thinking about how interesting the next three months will be working with Samantha. She's excellent at her job, but she sure is opinionated. Man!"

Lawrence shook his head. "I guess you would be the best person to call it. Takes one to know one as they say."

Joel frowned. "I'm not *that* opinionated."

"Yeah, whatever. So, did she say what she thought your chances were for going back to the fire department?"

"No. We didn't get to that, really. Plus, my doctor and the department will be the ones to make the call."

"Have you thought about Hightower Security at all? It could be—"

Oh, no, he was starting again. For the past four months, his family had been trying to get him to think about other options just in case he didn't get a clean bill of health to return to firefighting. He couldn't get them to understand he wasn't ready to consider other options.

He needed to believe he would be able to go back to the fire department.

"You know, I appreciate you taking your day off to go with me to my first physical therapy session, but I really don't want to talk about this. I just want to get better and get back to my normal life."

Lawrence nodded.

They watched the rest of the game in silence.

Samantha sat on her sofa, flipping the channels without a desire to really watch anything. After her horrendous day at work, she just wanted to veg out.

Joel Hightower was *nothing* like she had imagined him.

Why did that bother her? It shouldn't have. He was a patient.

She'd dealt with difficult patients before. As a professional, she just had to do her job.

When her phone started ringing, she contemplated not answering it. She wasn't in the mood for talking, especially if it was her mother on the other line.

She glanced at the caller ID. Seeing it was her friend, Jenny, the receptionist from the clinic, she picked up.

"Hey, girl. What's up?"

"Girl, I had to leave before you were done with your last patient." Jenny's bubbly voice came through the phone line. "And you *know* I had to call you and find out how it went. I've never seen you almost snap on a patient before. Girl, I thought you were going to rip his head off. His fine-as-he-wants-to-be head off, I might add."

Samantha hissed. "He's rude, and he's a bear."

And truth be told, his stank attitude hurt your feelings and shattered all the little idealized images of him you had in your mind.

"Whatever. He's something to look at, and he had his other fine brother with him." The distinct sound of smacking lips followed by "mmm" interrupted Jenny's adulation. "Girl, I was glad you were late. I got to sneak glances at those two fine Hightower men the entire time. You know, I went to high school with the oldest Hightower brother, Patrick. Every girl in Paterson wanted to snag one of those Hightower boys—"

"I can hardly imagine why. Joel Hightower is a surly, opinionated jerk. In fact, I'm going to start calling him Mr. Surly."

Jenny laughed.

"What're you laughing at? It's not funny."

"I just think it's funny you find him so opinionated. Tell me, is that your expert opinion, since you can be a little opinionated yourself?"

"Ha, ha, ha. The difference is my opinions are usually right, and his… Oh, forget it. I don't want to talk about Mr. Surly."

"Hmm… I've never seen you get this worked up over a guy before. Interesting."

"And I think you might be in need of a shrink, because clearly you've lost your mind."

"Right. We'll see what the next months shall bring, now won't we?"

"No, we won't, and I'm not worked up over Joel Hightower. I don't get worked up. That's not my style. I'm an easygoing, laid back, live and let live kind of a girl."

It was all she could do to keep her voice calm because she didn't like the fact that Jenny had called her on her less-than-cool response to the surly but fine-as-all-get-out Joel Hightower.

"Yeah, you're easygoing, all right. You easily let some of the finest men in North Jersey go on about their business once they get tired of trying to work their way into your world."

Samantha also didn't like the tone of Jenny's know-it-all voice that was hitting a little too close to home. So what if she hadn't met a guy who could successfully hold her interest for more than three dates? So what if she preferred to keep her options open and not get too serious at this point in her life?

"Oh, please tell me this isn't going to turn into another why-don't-you-settle-down talk. I like my life the way it is. I'm twenty-seven, I have a career I love, and I get to meet all kinds of guys and go out when I have time. I'm cool with my life." Was that a little whine in her voice she heard? She cleared her throat and sat up a little as she clutched the phone.

"You don't let anyone get close."

"I let you get close, and believe me, I rethink that every day," Samantha joked through tight lips.

"Ha, ha. You know that's not what I mean. If I didn't know you better, I might start to think you don't like men, but I think you just don't trust them. You're a serial dater, and you don't let guys stick around long enough to get close."

"That's not true!" *Not really…*

"What about my cousin Paul?"

"Paul? The cop?" Samantha shook her head as she remembered the brash rookie cop. He had been handsome without a doubt, but not handsome enough to make her forget her vow.

"Not my type. You shouldn't have even set me up with him. I could have told you that wasn't going to work. I'm not into guys with dangerous occupations."

"Mmm, hmm, and all other guys fit under the two-or-three date rule. You cut them loose after a few dates."

"That's because I'm particular about things like, oh, I don't know, *conversation.* I'm looking for someone who will make me think, make me laugh and who has a nice, *safe,* uneventful job. I'm not picky at all."

"So, you'll just keep dating and leaving all the most eligible guys in the area until there are no more left to date, without really giving them a chance?" Jenny's tone was exasperated.

"If they don't fit the criteria, I have to keep it moving. Time waits for no man, and neither do I. No need dragging out the inevitable. I prefer to think of it as power dating until I find the right one."

She blinked when Joel Hightower's bold and daring face popped into her head. Those brooding brown eyes would challenge her without end. That insufferable personality wouldn't allow him to agree with a thing she said and would probably make conversations riveting and interesting, to say the least. And those irritatingly witty little snipes of his would keep her on her toes. She tried to shake his smirking face from her head.

When that didn't work, she imagined him in his fireman uniform. The image didn't disappear, but at least it reminded her that no matter how much she found herself oddly attracted to him, he was not the one.

"And I think you might have met the right one today if you don't wimp out and give the sexy Hightower a fair look."

Samantha rolled her eyes toward the ceiling. What was it with Jenny and this Joel Hightower guy?

"*Whatever,* girlfriend." She yawned. "Listen, I'll see you tomorrow. Bye."

"Bye, Hightower Fan-Club President…"

Samantha sucked her teeth, hung up the phone and tried to get Joel Hightower out of her head.

The next morning, the phone woke Samantha up. She glanced at the clock. Seven o'clock. It was time to get up and start getting ready for work, anyway, but dang.

She cleared her throat and tried to do a halfway decent job of getting the frog out. "Hello."

"Hello, Sammie, did I wake you?"

"No, Mom." She tried to clear the cobwebs from her brain so she could get a read on her mother's voice. It was too early in the morning for Veronica Dash to be drunk, but that had never stopped her before. More than likely, she was getting an early start to her drinking day.

"I figured I would catch you before you went to that little job of yours. When I call you in the evenings, you never really have anything to say."

That's because the only thing I want to say to you is "Mom, stop drinking," but I can't say that because then you'd get all huffy and drink even more.

"Anyway, I know you were just home a few months back, but that was only for a week and a half. I just think it would be nice if you got a job in Chicago, or at least a little closer. So, I was looking through the want ads—"

"Mom, I'm happy with my job now. I like it here. You had to know I couldn't stay in Chicago forever."

This Samantha-come-home conversation was getting old.

"You act like it's so horrible for a mother to want her child closer to home."

Why? You haven't really paid me any attention since I was twelve and your drinking spiraled out of control.

But she couldn't say anything without starting World War III and sending her mother on a drinking binge.

Today, she opted out instead.

"When are you going to stop these little games of yours, Samantha? When are you going to stop or trying to punish me?"

Samantha sucked her teeth. Her mother would be the one to paint herself as the victim.

"Mom, I am not trying to punish you. I have a life and a career. I'm just trying to live my life, that's all."

"You're trying to punish me by staying away. Just like when you were a snotty little kid, who thought she could hurt someone by walking around not talking… Hmmph… Like I needed to hear you complain and tell me that I'd had enough to drink… What kind of child walks around the house for months, not speaking to her mother? I'll tell you what kind! A vin-

dictive little snot who's trying to punish the parent instead of staying in a child's place."

Enough of this!

"How about a child who is trying the best way she
can to get her mother to stop trying to kill herself with
a liquor bottle? Or one who was afraid she would say
something that would send her mother on yet *another*
drinking binge. Take your pick, Mom, because I've
been both!"

As soon as the words fell out of her mouth, she regretted them. The last thing she wanted to do was argue
with her mother. In fact, she avoided the battleground
at all costs most times. She ran her hand across her face
and finished wiping the sleep out of her eyes.

"Listen, I've got to go get ready for work, Mom.
I'll call you this weekend—"

"Don't bother!"

Click.

*Oh, yes… Getting hung up on by one's mother…
What a glorious way to start your day!*

Samantha softly laid the phone down and headed
for the shower.

"All I want to know is if I work hard enough and
do what I'm supposed to do in physical therapy, is
there a real chance that I can go back to firefighting?"
Joel tried to get a straight answer out of his doctor.

"And as I said, making your back stronger and getting the most out of physical therapy is what you need to be focusing on." Dr. Lardner kept his eyes on his pad.

"Also, the fire department's physician would be the one to give the final go-ahead about you going back to work. I will say that a back injury as extreme as yours will take a lot of work in order for a person to go back to such a physically demanding job."

Joel ran his hand across his head in frustration.

"And I'm asking you, if I put in the work needed, is it a possibility? I need to know that it's a possibility."

He hated the pleading sound in his voice, but holding on to the hope his life could go back to normal was the only thing keeping him going, keeping him positive. His family's quest to get him to see other options was starting to punch holes in his resolve.

"Honestly, when you came into the hospital with the injuries you had, I didn't think you would ever walk again. Luckily the damage didn't lead to paralysis, and you are walking on your own two feet today. So, I don't want to say with certainty you wouldn't be able to do what you needed to do to make your back stronger, strong enough to go back to firefighting, but I don't want to make any promises."

"That's okay. Just knowing there's a chance is good enough for me."

For now, until I can make it a reality and end up doing the job I love again.

The feeling he got from being able to rush into a blazing building head on—tackle and tame the burning flames until they were wiped out—was unlike anything he had ever felt. He remembered the first time he ever saw an out-of-control fire. It had been awe-inspiring. When he saw those firemen carry a little girl and her grandmother from the fire, he knew without a doubt that was what he wanted to do. While most little boys growing up at that time wanted to be Superman or Batman, he already knew what kind of superhero he wanted to be. He wanted to be a fireman. He still wanted to be a fireman.

"Oh, and, Doc, uh, I was wondering about…sex… with my back…" This had to be the most awkward conversation ever.

"You will certainly be able to have sex. You'll just have to be a little careful and not stress your back. Your physical therapist will be able to give you some advice on the best positions—"

"Aah…no." He tried to imagine having a conversation about back-friendly sex with Little Miss Spitfire, especially when he'd had some interesting dreams about the curvy, sexy and opinionated woman last night.

"I mean, she's a woman, and it would be awkward. Can you recommend some books or something?"

"I certainly can."

"Good." He hadn't become concerned with the topic of sex until now. He had a hint it might have something to do with the spark of desire he felt for Samantha Dash.

Chapter 3

After two-and-a half months of intense therapy, Joel had come to hate his sessions.

He didn't hate the sessions so much as what they represented: the ever-growing possibility he might never fight fires again.

Sure, they could make the pain manageable and most times nonexistent. He could even get on with a perfectly normal and boring regular life, but no matter how hard he worked, he couldn't seem to bring things back to the way they were before the accident. His back still wasn't strong enough to support the heavy equipment.

And then there was his physical therapist: Little

Miss Spitfire. It seemed as if she lived to disagree with everything he said.

One would think two black urban professionals would have more in common, especially when he felt an intense attraction to the woman unlike anything he'd ever felt before, and his attraction led him to the irony of ironies. The woman knew all about his injuries and therefore his limitations, and no man wanted to step to a woman when she already knew he wasn't bringing it the way he wanted to.

Forget that.

So for the past couple of months he'd been resisting. Resisting the urge to plant a kiss on those lips of fire. Resisting pulling the curvaceous body that could put Jennifer Hudson out of business into his arms. Resisting putting down his best lines and his tightest game to pull the most beautiful dark-chocolate goddess into his life.

And all the resisting kept a brother in a state of constant grumpiness.

When she finally came into the room, all bubbly and carrying those electric stimulation pads, he felt like smiling back at her, but all he could do was nod and grunt hello.

"Well, well, well, if it isn't my favorite curmudgeon." She laughed and it sounded like music—music he wanted to bottle up and keep.

He glanced at her. She was wearing her white lab coat over a light summer outfit. Her cream slacks were topped by a pastel pink-and-cream blouse. The twists she normally wore in her hair had been loosened and gave her jet-black hair a crinkly, curly effect.

He liked how she looked *way* too much.

Trying not to smile or laugh or otherwise let her know how much her simple presence brightened his day, he coolly asked, "Do you make a habit of insulting all your patients?"

"Nope, only the overly pleasant ones like you," she offered sarcastically.

He had to laugh at that.

"See, there's that million-dollar smile. You really ought to show it more often, Mr. Surly." She grinned and he noticed the soft gloss on her lips. It was a neutral shade with more shine than color, but with the flash of her perfect teeth she didn't need any color to highlight her smile.

Samantha Dash had the kind of smile that could make a man clean out his bank account and give her everything he owned just to see it.

"I would if you were always so pleasant and agreeable, Little Miss Spitfire."

She'd finally placed the electric stimulation patches on his back and started the treatments.

He grimaced as the small shocks did their job.

"Sometimes I think you get too much of a kick out of this."

"Who me? Never." She laughed her sweet bell-like laugh again.

He didn't know what worked better for his pain, the treatment or seeing her.

Seeing her.

After the treatment, they sat in her office, going over her plans for the rest of his treatments and discussing his progress.

He realized he had come a long way from where he was when he was injured during the big warehouse fire, but he still wasn't back on the job.

The people around him, from his doctors to his family, kept pushing him to consider what he would do if it never happened, if he could no longer fight fires. He didn't even want to think about those possibilities. Instead, he pushed them out of his mind and focused on his surroundings.

He had come to like her cozy little office. The only thing that didn't seem to fit her was the fake greenery in the room. She seemed like a real-plant kind of a girl.

There was nothing fake about her. From the tips of her natural hair, to each and every curve on her body, to the unapologetically real retorts that came out of her mouth, she proved time and time again she kept it real.

"So how is the pain? You have less than a month left of therapy. We've been at this for over two months, are you noticing any difference? It definitely looks like your range of motion and strength are improving."

"Yes, the pain isn't as bad. In fact, sometimes I can go weeks without a flare-up."

"That's wonderful." She smiled, and he could have sworn the entire office lit up.

He felt a stirring in his heart, and it shot straight to his groin. He couldn't believe out of all the women he had come into contact with since his accident, he would find himself growing increasingly and overwhelmingly attracted to the one woman who knew all his shortcomings.

When he'd first become injured, he pretty much pushed the women he'd been casually dating away, at least the ones that tried to stick around and came to visit him in the hospital. He told himself that he didn't need any pity, and he still firmly believed that. He also didn't want anything taking his focus away from making his back stronger and returning to his job.

He hadn't even missed the female companionship. In fact, the entire time he spent confined in the hospital, the only thing he really missed was his job. Then he came to physical therapy… Seeing Samantha three times a week seemed to add heat to parts of him he'd thought were frozen. His emotions were thawing, and he liked it.

He shrugged and tried to play nonchalant.

"You don't look pleased." She squinted her big, bold, brown eyes and studied him a bit too closely for his taste.

"I'd be more pleased if I could go back to doing what I was born to do."

She inhaled and nodded. "You do realize how lucky you are, though, don't you? You could have died in that fire. Or your back injuries could have been such that you could have been permanently paralyzed, but you're alive. You're healthy. You can walk without aid. You just have a sensitive back, one you will have to take care not to aggravate or reinjure."

Joel bristled at her sharp tone.

"Well, don't hold back now, sweetheart. Tell me how you really feel." He leaned back in his chair.

As he took her in, he realized his chocolate beauty was probably thanking heaven her delicious dark skin wouldn't show any signs of blushing. She looked really cute when she was contrite, and he found himself enjoying her uneasy stance.

"I'm sorry. I don't usually give my opinion in this manner with patients. You can, of course, feel anyway you wish. I just wanted to highlight that you really have a lot to be thankful for…" Her voice faltered off.

"Oh, your point is very much noted, *Ms*. Dash."

He watched her back straighten and her hand absently twirled her hair. She sucked her bottom lip in and nibbled on it for a moment, and in that moment he wished he were her teeth. He wanted to nibble and suck on those lips with an intensity that caused him to shift and squirm a bit to contain his urge to lean over and plant one on her.

In that very moment, he realized he was going to have Little Miss Spitfire soon. No matter what.

She took a deep breath and stood. "So, I guess I'll see you Friday then. Your next appointment is in the evening, right?" She walked over to her office door.

He followed her with a pep in his step he hadn't felt since the accident. There was something about coming to a realization, an understanding with oneself you'd been trying to fight or deny that rejuvenated one's energy.

Giving in to the inevitable almost felt like a brick wall being lifted from his spirit, a shackle being broken from his soul. It felt like freedom.

It felt like a challenge he knew he would rise to and conquer. Because knowledge of his injuries and their many differences aside, Miss Samantha Dash's lips demanded to be kissed and her thick bodacious body needed to be held.

By him!

Little Miss Spitfire had heated things up, and he was just the man to show her how to really make it hot.

"Argh!" Samantha sank into her seat and groaned in disgust.

She hadn't meant to go off on her patient the way she did, but the sexy Joel Hightower brought out things in her she usually kept contained and under wraps.

Sure, she thought of snappy things to say and had some funny wisecracks running through her head all the time, but she had never voiced them before. Not with a patient. She had always been content to think them and make herself laugh—until Joel.

Growing up not being able to always tell her mother the things she was thinking had conditioned her to let all the things she wanted to say filter through her head and censor before she said them. Most times, she kept her smart comments and wisecracks to herself. It was enough to just come up with the zingers. Since meeting Joel Hightower, she had been letting her thoughts and opinions run freer than ever.

And what was with her telling him he should be thankful he's alive and could walk? Even if she did firmly believe he should, she would have never crossed the professional line in the past.

Chastising a patient? That was a big no-no.

She leaned back in her chair and started to play with her hair. She needed to wash it and retwist it.

She had been wearing her hair in its natural state for several years now and had started to wear her shoulder-length, jet-black hair in two-strand twists as she flirted with the idea of locking her hair permanently.

The door to her office came bursting open, and she glanced up. Jenny needed to learn how to knock.

"I noticed our finest patient just left. That man is yummy to look at."

She rolled her eyes at Jenny. "Does your husband know you spend your days ogling handsome patients?"

"Oh, so you finally acknowledge he's handsome? Interesting." A knowing smirk crossed Jenny's lips as the older woman took a seat.

"I didn't acknowledge a thing. He's *a'right*. He's not all that." She sighed.

Shoot, Joel Hightower was more than all that. He was all that and then some…and then some more on top of that!

The only problem was she wasn't supposed to notice how fine he was. The man was off-limits.

"Right, all I know is he is lucky I'm a married woman. He might have a stalker on his hands. That man is movie-star handsome. Goodness gracious!" Jenny patted her chest in mock-lust.

"Girl, stop. You know you wrong for that. You're the one married to the Denzel Washington look-alike."

If Samantha didn't know Jenny was madly in love with her handsome husband, Walt, she might have been worried. But she had spent enough time with the couple and their two beautiful children to know that, as much smack as Jenny talked, she would never act on it.

Even though Jenny and her husband, Walt, were about ten years Samantha's senior, she considered them to be good friends. She didn't know what she would do without Jenny in the clinic to laugh and commiserate with. Having another sister there was comforting, and they hit it off from day one.

"Girl, my Denzel look-alike is fine, but every now and then a new youngster comes around and makes you take notice. And that one that just left here…" Jenny fanned herself. "Girl, you better snap him up."

She shook her head, laughing at her friend's antics, and Jenny started laughing, too.

"He's a patient. That's unprofessional."

"Girl, please. He won't be a patient for long. Remember, I file the charts. He has less than a month left, and you need to start putting things in place for when he's no longer coming here three times a week." Jenny rolled her eyes. "And last I checked, there weren't any rules against you dating a former patient."

"He's *still* a patient. Anyway, it's unprofessional.

I can't do it. I try to be as professional as I can be at all times."

"Mmm… Well, professional isn't gonna keep you warm at night, and professional isn't easy on the eyes like Joel Hightower. In my opinion, professional is highly overrated if it means you have to pass on a man like that. I saw the way he looks at you… Girl, that man eyes you as if he wants to sop you up with a biscuit."

"Stop lying, Jenny. He does no such thing."

"You wanna put some money on it?"

"No, I don't. I wouldn't put money on something like that. Plus, a man as fine as him could have and *probably does* have any woman he wants. He probably likes those skinny model chicks."

Samantha was more than happy with her curvy figure and had no desire to move from her size twelve to a size two, but, she knew not every man could handle a sister with some meat on the bones.

"What he wants is you, and I wonder what you're gonna do when he decides to go after what he wants."

"I don't think we have to worry about that happening." But Samantha couldn't help letting herself wonder what if…

What if Joel Hightower really wanted her? The heat rose to her neck, her face flushed and her heart started to flutter. Why now?

After years of being able to go with the flow and date guys without getting caught up in emotions… After years of staying clear of men with dangerous occupations… After years of being professional and not crossing the line with anyone she was treating…

Why was Joel Hightower able to tempt her with a smile and a look? Why was he the one to cause her desire to bubble over and need she had barely known she had to erupt? Most importantly, why was she starting to believe she wasn't going to be able to continue doing things the way she had been doing them. After years of steering clear of the dangers that came with falling in love, she seemed to be primed and ready to make the leap right into Joel Hightower's arms. And that scared her as much as it excited her.

Chapter 4

After her last appointment of the day, Samantha made it home to her apartment in Elmwood Park in record time.

The town she lived in, Elmwood Park, had started out many years ago as a sort of suburb of Paterson, like South Paterson and West Paterson. In fact, the town used to be called East Paterson until they changed the name to remove all associations with the inner city. Still, it was a little safer for a single woman living on her own. Also, her apartment complex was nice and welcoming.

And she never felt happier to see the red-and-white

brick, colonial-style apartment units than she was today. She pulled into her parking spot, thinking about what she could quickly make for dinner. Her phone was ringing as she walked through the door, and she rushed to answer it.

It better not be a telemarketer, she thought as she made the dash across the living room/dining room to the phone hanging on the back wall of her galley kitchen.

"Hey, Sammie. It's your mother." Veronica Dash's soft voice wafted through the phone lines, and Samantha tried to discern what kind of mood she was in.

Was it her sober and depressed mother on the line, her two-glasses-of-gin shy of passing out and depressed mother or her angry, bitter, lashing-out and drunk mother?

"Hi, Mom. How's it going?"

"When are you coming home? Why can't you get a job here in Chicago? What kind of daughter leaves her mother all alone?" The slight slur in her voice canceled out still sober.

Samantha started walking with the cordless phone, kicking off her shoes and making herself comfortable on the huge plush brown sofa-sectional that took up the majority of the small living room/dining room. There was no telling how long she would be on the phone with her mother this evening.

She could hear the sound of clanging glass and knew Veronica must have been fixing herself another drink.

"Mom, I have a job here that I love, and I like it here. You could always move out here. A change of scenery might be good for you." She had made the offer many times before, and she knew her mother would turn it down.

Samantha loved Chicago and would always consider herself a Chi-town girl. But when she left home to attend graduate school and earn her MS in Occupational Therapy at Seton Hall University in South Orange, New Jersey, she ended up staying on for the DPT—Doctor of Physical Therapy—program. By the time she finished her studies, she'd come to love the North Jersey area, and she had come to love the new-found peace in her life and not having to watch her mother drink herself to death.

Finally, she had a legitimate reason to leave the continuous sadness looming in her childhood home. As much as it shamed her to admit it, she was sort of glad her mother didn't want to move to New Jersey.

"I'm all alone, and I don't want to leave my home. It's all I have left of him. It's the *only* thing I have left. If you were any kind of a daughter, you wouldn't have left me. How could you leave here? We're a family here."

"You have me. The house is just a place, Mom. You

have me, also. Daddy was murdered but you still have me…" Samantha wished she could call back the words as soon as they left her mouth.

"I don't have you. You're not here. You're no help. You're selfish. You're trying to punish me because you think it will make me stop drinking. Just like when you stopped visiting. Cutting me off… Selfish!"

Samantha closed her eyes. She didn't say anything because her mother was right. She had tried to use the threat of not visiting as a ploy to get her mother to go to rehab in the past. It hadn't worked.

"They murdered him. They took him away from me. Why? Why did he stop at that corner store to pick up cough medicine for you? It's your fault. It's your fault my husband is dead." Veronica's angry words caused Samantha to go still.

It wasn't as if she hadn't heard the words before. It was more that she was shocked that they still had the ability to wound.

Samantha spoke so she could barely hear her own words. "It wasn't my fault. It was the criminal's fault, the one who was robbing the store when Daddy walked in."

In the past, Samantha might have been spiteful enough to add that she wasn't the one who called her husband and asked him to pick up a bottle of Robitussin while he was on duty. But the grown-up woman knew it was no more her fault than it was her mother's.

"Mom, maybe you shouldn't have another drink tonight. I know thinking about Daddy makes you sad—"

"You never loved your father, Samantha. You always resented the fact that he had a job to do protecting the city and the fact that he didn't make it home in time and he missed a couple of your little birthday parties, but he was a cop and he had a job to do. He couldn't just be home with you all the time, and they killed him. They took him away from me." A tortured sob escaped Veronica's mouth, and the sound of it pierced Samantha's heart.

"Mom, I loved Daddy very much. You really shouldn't have another drink tonight. It's making you sad. Try to remember the happy times. He was a good man, a good father and a good husband—"

"Your father would be so disappointed in you, Sammie. So disappointed. You're selfish, and he'd be disappointed. You're supposed to be here, taking care of me now that he's gone. He always took such good care of me. He loved his Roni. He loved me so much." Her words slurred together and they tapered off.

Samantha heard a small crash and assumed it was her mother's phone hitting the floor. Worried Veronica had fallen, too, she was about to hang up and call

Chicago's emergency services when her mother picked up the phone.

"I'm tired now, Sammie. I'll talk to you later."

The dial tone sounded so abrupt. She closed her eyes and leaned her head back on the arm of the sofa. She felt drained.

She never understood how a woman could love a man so much losing him would literally make her stop living her own life, but she had watched it with her own eyes.

Joel entered the sports bar and looked around for his brothers. He'd promised he would meet them there, but a part of him wanted to back out. He loved his brothers, and he cherished the time he spent with them, but after the accident, it was just too hard to be around them. Their lives were still exciting, and they were living up to the Hightower creed of honor and service.

Jason and Lawrence were police detectives with the Paterson police department and his oldest brother, Patrick, had just been promoted to captain in the fire department. Joel had hoped to one day make captain himself. He had to keep working hard to make sure his dream came true and he would be able to fight fires again. He couldn't allow himself to think about what he'd do if it wasn't a possibility.

He walked over to their booth and tried to shake

off the negative feelings. He thought of Little Miss Spitfire and smiled.

Samantha was right about one thing; he was lucky to be alive. He would heal and go back to the job he loved. He had to.

His brothers stood, and they all hugged in greeting.

His youngest brother, Jason, seemed to practically glow with happiness. His smile was almost contagious. Jason, a cold-case detective, used to give their older brother, Patrick, a run for his money when it came to sulkiness. *Marriage must really agree with Jason.* He had reunited with his high-school sweetheart, former video dancer, Penny Keys. Their love was solid.

Joel was happy for them. The accident had made him angry and bitter, but not so bitter he couldn't be genuinely happy for Jason and Penny.

Lawrence, a narcotics detective, gave him a quick hug and then leaned back into his seat in the booth. Of all the Hightower brothers, Lawrence was the most educated and also the most street savvy. His master's degree in criminology could have easily been a diploma from the school of hard knocks if he had taken a different path, or perhaps if he hadn't had the Hightower name to live up to. When they were boys, Lawrence was the only one of their parents' sons who seemed poised to rebuke the legacy. He flirted with the wild side, but ended up on the right side of the tracks. His bad-boy streak probably helped him a lot in his job.

Patrick's quick hug and pound was atypical for the eldest Hightower son. Patrick hadn't been the same since he found his wife in the bed with another man. The breakup of his marriage and an ugly divorce had left Patrick cold. He had never been the most affectionate person, but now he was even more guarded. No doubt from fear of being hurt again. He held his feelings back constantly.

"So, how's everything, man?" Jason asked with a grin on his face.

Joel smiled. "Everything's cool. I can't complain." He shrugged. "I'm alive."

Both Patrick and Lawrence gave him a funny look. Even Jason stared at him.

"What? What are you all looking at me like I'm crazy for? I'm good. It's all good." Joel slid into the booth. He noticed they were still giving him those weird, scared glances, and he regretted even trying to be his normal joking, upbeat self. "What? I was joking, sheesh."

"Well, it's not funny, man." Jason's happy-go-lucky expression soured.

"Yeah, and I don't buy that joke crap, by the way. Are you okay? How's everything, really, man? And don't give us that bull about it all being good. You almost died, and it took a lot just to have you walking again. You might not be able to go back to the fire department, and that was your life. How're you, really, man?" Lawrence cut right to the chase.

Joel flinched. "Well, when you put it that way, I guess it's not all good. Damn, man, you ever heard of holding back? Good thing you aren't in crisis negotiation. You'd have a person jumping from the ledge or all the hostages would be dead by the time you were done."

Jason and Patrick laughed, while Lawrence ran his had across his head in reflection.

Joel could tell that Lawrence had a lot he wanted to say for weeks now. Things must really be bad if his normally cool brother let it blow the way he did. Whatever Lawrence had held back for the past few weeks, clearly he had no intention holding on now.

Joel sincerely hoped Lawrence would back off. He didn't know how much more of his brothers' inquiries—no matter how well intentioned they seemed to be—he could take.

"Seriously, Joel, we're worried about you. You've been pretty silent these past few months. And we've been trying to give you time to talk about stuff when you got ready, but your therapy is almost over, and you still haven't talked about the fact that—"

Nope, Lawrence was letting it all hang out, so Joel had to cut him off.

Joel slammed his hand on the table in an effort to let his brother know he'd had enough. "The fact that I might never fight fires again? The fact that my back will more than likely never be the same and I'll be battling back pain the rest of my life?" He was holding his jaw so tight every single word he said came out stressed.

He should have canceled. He wasn't ready for this.

"Could it simply be that I don't want to dwell on the negative?" Again he bit out his words with a barely contained rage. The nerve of them trying to pull some kind of intervention on him! Didn't they realize he was doing the best he could given the circumstances?

"That's all fine and well, but you can't just keep stuff like that all bottled in, bro, and there's a big difference between not dwelling on the negative and being in denial," Patrick offered.

Joel gritted his teeth to keep from cursing. *This is bull.* Patrick was the last person who needed to be calling anyone out for keeping things inside.

And so what if he was keeping things inside? Did any of them know what it was like to feel like half the man he used to be? Did any of them have the one thing they had always wanted to be, ever since they were a kid and got their first little fire truck Matchbox car cruelly snatched away from them? Were either one of them faced with the real possibility that he would never be the man he was again because the self-identity that he had crafted and nurtured over the years was gone?

No. They didn't. So as far as he was concerned, they couldn't tell him jack.

"We know how much firefighting means to you. That's why we're concerned," Lawrence offered.

"You don't know anything about it, and if you're lucky, you'll never have to know," Joel snapped.

"I know how I'd feel if I couldn't fight fires anymore," Patrick stated solemnly. "I'd feel like a big chunk of myself was missing. I might even be dumb enough to question my worth, but hopefully you three would step in and help me see that I'm so much more than my job and I have a lot more to offer the world even if I can't fight fires anymore."

"That's easy for you to say, *Captain!*" Joel's words came out snidely and he didn't like the sound of his voice. He just knew he wasn't ready for this. Why couldn't they see that and just leave it alone?

"We're just worried about you, man. So what's going on?" Jason chimed in.

"How is your back?" Lawrence asked.

"Are you going to at least explore the option of taking a position with Dad at Hightower Security?" Patrick wore an oddly hopeful expression.

Joel inhaled so deeply his nostrils flared. An angry hiss of breath escaped his lips. Their little intervention became increasingly more annoying because he realized even though he didn't have all the answers to their questions, what he did have he wasn't so sure he wanted to face yet. He counted to ten and then counted again.

He stood and glared at each of his brothers. "I can't do this tonight." Those were the only words he trusted himself to say, as angry as he was, he didn't want to say anything that couldn't be taken back or apologized for later.

His brothers all glanced at one another, and he could see the wheels spinning in their heads as they tried to think of ways to keep him there.

"Hey, look, bro, we'll back off. Sit back down. You don't have to talk about it if you don't want to. We just wanted to see you," Lawrence offered.

"Yeah, who knows when Jason here will have another free night away from Penny. Pulling him away from the old ball and chain is like pulling teeth." Patrick let out a nervous chuckle.

"That's not true. It's not like pulling teeth." A sly smile covered Lawrence's mouth as he waved his hand in mock disagreement. "Pulling teeth is *much* easier than getting Jason to leave Penny's side."

His older brothers started laughing, and Jason frowned.

Joel started to walk away from the table. It was better to walk away than stay there in his current mood and end up taking it out on his brothers. It wasn't their fault.

Jason reached out and grabbed Joel's arm. Joel snatched it back in reflex before pausing to calm himself.

"Hey, man, you can't leave me here alone to deal with these two clowns. Stay a little while," Jason stated in a mock pleading tone.

Joel inhaled and exhaled trying to find the somewhat positive mood he'd come in with before sitting back down. He figured he might as well stay for a minute and make it the younger Hightower brothers versus the oldest brothers. Like the good old days.

"So how is married life treating you, baby bro?" he asked Jason.

Jason gave Lawrence and Patrick the evil eye before turning his attention to Joel. "It's wonderful, man. My only regret is that we wasted so many years."

Joel nodded. Jason and Penny belonged together. He wondered if he'd ever find the woman who would complete him and light fire to his soul the way Penny did for Jason. No sooner than he thought it did the feisty chocolate beauty Samantha Dash pop into his mind.

His pulse quickened, and for the first time in a long time, he felt a rush. Now, there was a woman who could bring out passion in a man. So what if he couldn't seem to agree with a word that came out of her mouth, her full, luscious, delectable mouth. The image of her beautiful lips planted itself in his brain, and for the rest of the evening with his brothers all he could do was think of what it would be like to kiss them. How did they taste? Now more than ever, he was determined to find out.

Chapter 5

It had to be the worst session with a patient Samantha had ever had. The most god-awful encounter with another person she had ever experienced in her twenty-seven years on the planet. And the closest she had ever come to physically hurting another human being.

But Joel Hightower was behaving in a less-than-human manner and giving off more attitude than usual. Since she had vowed not to lose her professionalism and snap at him again, she tried to grin and bear it.

However, him standing there, smirking at her as she tried to show him new stretching exercises broke her resolve. She could have sworn he was trying to provoke her. She went off.

"Do you not want to be able to cope with the pain? Am I boring you, Mr. Hightower? Or maybe you just like the pain?" She put her hand on her hip and glared at him.

For the first time that afternoon, her grumpy patient smiled. At least, it looked like a smile and less like the smart-aleck, condescending smirk he'd been wearing.

"What's your deal, Joel? I can only help you if you let me. Would you like to change to a different therapist for your final month?"

Ready to throw in the towel didn't even begin to touch how she felt. It was hard enough seeing him three times a week and getting glimpses of that funny, sweet guy she had imagined him to be before she actually met him. When Joel Hightower wasn't putting on his sulking front, he was actually quite charming, too darn charming.

He frowned then. "No. I want to keep you. It's just…I'm not sure this is worth it. I still may not be able to do the job I love."

She took a deep breath. Now was not the time to force him to see he could find other jobs he loved because he was still alive to do so. Instead she took a seat on the mat and looked up at him.

Squinting, she contemplated the best approach.

Typically, she would offer a pep talk and finish guiding her patient on the path to recovery from a professional distance, but when she gazed up in his sincere but stressed brown eyes, she couldn't maintain her distance.

She swallowed as she realized she cared about Joel Hightower. And even if she wasn't ready to admit it let alone give into it, she knew she had to give in to her need to comfort him.

Leaning back against the wall, she patted the spot on the mat next to her. Joel didn't hesitate at all and took a seat.

"Would not being able to fight fires anymore be the absolute worst thing that could happen?"

"Yes." He didn't even pause before answering her.

And more important, he barely left any room for her to encourage him to open up more.

"Would you rather be dead than to not be able to fight fires? Because I can tell you this, the people you would leave behind wouldn't want that. Your family and friends would rather have you here."

He paused then, and she wondered if his silence signaled she had overstepped her bounds with him. She seemed to have become good at doing that.

"When I was a kid, I would watch all of the men in my family—my father, his cousins, all of them, in their uniforms. The cops, the firemen… There's the

Hightower legacy of service that we get taught almost
from the crib, but there is also growing up and seeing
the men in our family do their thing." He stopped, and
silence rang through the air. She had no desire to fill
it. It seemed too precious, the build-up too great. She
let out her breath slowly. She hadn't realized she had
been holding it.

"So much of what you grow up thinking a *man* is,
is all tied to the uniform, the badges… So yes, when
I woke up in the hospital and realized that I might not
be able to fight fires again…to wear the uniform…to
be a man…a Hightower man…I thought it would
have been better to just be dead."

She gasped, and a chill ran through her blood. She
couldn't stand the thought that Joel at one time considered death a better option than life.

"My dad was a police officer with the Chicago police department. He was murdered trying to stop a
robbery in a corner store when I was twelve." Her
shaky voice surprised both of them.

"I'm sorry to hear that. There are really no words
to say…" Joel's words faltered off.

"He worked a lot, and I didn't get to spend a whole
lot of time with him, but the little time I did spend
with him, he made special. I was such a daddy's girl.
During basketball season, he would always find time
to take me to a few Bulls games, and from the time I

was around six years old, we would have a father-and-daughter day and he'd take me out to eat and we'd just bond. When I was twelve, my last year before he was murdered… He told me that he was showing me how a respectable guy is supposed to treat a lady so I'd know…" She cleared her throat. She couldn't continue.

Joel placed his arm around her shoulder, and her entire body heated up and tingled before a calm came over her.

"It's not better to be dead, Joel. Not for the people you leave behind, and as heroic and manly as it must make people feel to be able to put on a uniform and save lives, I know that I adored and worshiped the man that used to take me to games, make me laugh and shower me with love way more than I did the cop in a uniform."

"But you do know that your dad was a hero and he died doing something he had dedicated himself to doing—fighting crime and saving lives. The police force is a noble tradition and it takes great men to really do that shield justice." He paused, and a rueful smile crossed his lips.

"If you ever meet any of my brothers, don't you dare tell them I said that. I'd never hear the end of it. Two of my brothers are cops and my dad was a cop, too."

"I know he was a hero. He was a brave man, and I miss him." She shifted and cleared her throat again. "So, enough about me. This is supposed to be about you." She tried for a lighthearted laugh that didn't quite make it. "What has you in such a funk today… besides your usual surly nature?"

He chuckled. "I guess I've been wondering what will happen if I can't be a fireman anymore. I don't know what…"

The hesitation and uncertainty in his voice caused the lightbulb to go off in her head. "You don't know what you're going to do now?"

"Sort of. My father retired early from the Paterson police department. He'd invested well and made enough money to start his own company, Hightower Security. It specializes in all aspects of making folks feel secure—from alarm systems to actual security guards. He provides inspection services, the whole deal, and my brothers and I all own a piece of the company and always envisioned working there once we became too old to do what we're doing now or just needed a change."

Samantha nodded. It felt good to finally feel as if she had some insight to the man. "And you feel like you're being put out to pasture too soon?"

"Dang, girl! Subtlety is definitely not your strong point."

Joel started laughing, and she felt the heat rise from her neck to her cheeks.

Since when did she turn into Sammie-blush-a-lot?

Since she met up with Joel Hightower, that's when.

"You look so cute when you do that." His voice got really deep, and she turned to look at him against her better judgment.

Goodness, the man was fine. His expressive brown eyes and smooth, sexy smile made his handsome face shine. She'd never seen a man more good-looking, not even on a movie screen. He had the kind of gaze a girl could get lost in: one part serious, two parts sensuous and one part sexy as all get out. That face and his muscular frame combined with the underlying playful and very devilish manner equaled danger to any sane and breathing girl's heart. It certainly had the warning buzzers going off in her head.

So why wasn't she listening to them? *Proceed with caution, hell!* She kept right on falling into the dark chocolate pools that made up his eyes.

She tilted her head and tried to give off the impression she wasn't scared. "Do what?"

"Get all nervous and embarrassed and start blushing." He smiled, and she could have sworn she saw a sparkle.

"You can't see me blush, Hightower. My complexion doesn't allow for that." She smirked even as she wondered how he could possibly know that if she were a few shades lighter, she would be lit up like Rudolph's nose on Christmas Eve.

"Oh, maybe I can't see it, but I know it. I can tell. You're nervous and curious all at the same time."

"Yeah, well, we all know what too much curiosity did to the cat…" She let out a sigh.

"True, but we also know satisfaction revived the little feline in the *best* way."

Was that a sexy taunt she heard in the undertone of his voice?

"Who's to say I'd be satisfied if I gave in to my curiosity?" She felt way more saucy than she had a right to given he was a patient, but that didn't stop the hint of a pant in her voice.

She needed to quit it. She really did.

A sinful, sexy smile crossed his lips. "If you're curious about what I *know* you're curious about then I can promise you heights of satisfaction unlike anything you have ever experienced."

There it was again. There was no mistaking the sensuous taunt.

She made the dreaded mistake of looking up into his intense stare and the truth of his promise nearly took her breath away. He meant it, all right. He met her gaze without blinking.

"Well…" She wiped her suddenly sweating palms on her slacks and got up from the mat.

He followed, and she noticed him wince a little.

"I'm going to show you these stretching exercises and you are going to follow, and then I'm going to give you a heat treatment. And when you come in here on Monday, you are going to leave that funky attitude at the door. Because if you don't, I will be forced to bring out the big guns."

He grinned. "Oh, I'm going to be on my best behavior from now on. My new mission is to make you throw caution to the wind, little kitten, and to give us both some satisfaction. I'm glad you took it upon yourself to take me to task today, Little Miss Spitfire. I'm feeling things I haven't felt in a long time, and I know I want to feel more, *much more*." His tone went down a couple of notches, and his voice became Barry White deep and sexy.

Her knees suddenly felt weak, and she wanted to flop back down on the mat.

What had she gotten herself into?

She should have kept her professional distance because Joel Hightower's big predator cat on the prowl was *way* out of her league. He could satisfy his curiosity all he wanted and he'd end up fine, but how much would she have to risk in order to play his game? And how would she be able to resist?

* * *

Getting in his SUV, Joel replayed what had happened in his therapy session with a smile on his face. He wondered if Little Miss Spitfire even realized he had thrown down the gauntlet. He shook his head and chuckled to himself.

No, she probably had no idea.

The slight soreness in his back reminded him he wasn't one hundred percent, and he probably never would be. It bothered him almost enough to make him consider not pursuing Samantha. Could he ever be the man she'd want him to be?

Then he thought about how she understood him without even trying, how she took pushing him to get better and went way past her job as his therapist. He could tell she wasn't like that with all her patients. More than anything else, verbally sparring with her the past couple of months offered a thrill and excitement he hadn't felt in a long time, and that was something he wasn't ready to give up.

Samantha sat in her office, staring into space, wondering exactly what had happened between herself and Joel. One minute she was in total control and the consummate professional, and the next…the next… What?

She groaned and absently twisted her hair.

"That doesn't sound like a woman who just spent a couple of hours with the finest man in the city, next to my Walt."

Samantha glanced up and rolled her eyes at Jenny. "I see you switched up your song. I'm *still* telling your husband you're up in here eyeing strange men."

"Girl, it ain't nothing strange about that Hightower boy. So what happened today? He left here grinning from ear to ear."

"That's because he's full of the devil." Samantha pursed her lips in deep thought. Shaking her head to clear it from the image of Joel's handsome smiling face, she stood.

"Girl, you best just sit back down and tell me all about your visit with Mr. Manly Man. You two have taken the place of my soaps. I don't even tape *All My Children* anymore. I've got all your business to keep me full of suspense and drama." She started talking in a fake announcer's voice. "Will the beautiful Samantha Dash be brave enough to take on the stunningly handsome and sexy Joel Hightower? Tune in every Monday, Wednesday and Friday to see if she will get the hint that—"

"Okay, Jenny, dang!" Samantha shook her head and started laughing. "You just won't quit."

"Well, at least you're not wasting your breath trying to convince me he doesn't like you. Come on, spill it, girl. I ain't got all day. This was your last appointment of the day and y'all stayed in here an extra twenty minutes. I should have been left for the day."

"You could have left because I have nothing to tell you, girlfriend."

"Aww! Come on now, Samantha. I've got five minutes before I need to get out of here and pick up the kids from their after-school programs. I have to beat the traffic on Route 80. Spill, girl, I don't have all day."

She laughed at Jenny's distressed expression. "There's nothing to tell. Go get your kids."

"Okay, I lied. Walt is picking up the kids today. Spill." Jenny took a seat and bounced up and down in anticipation.

"It's official, Jenny. You're crazy. *So* crazy." Samantha sunk back in her own chair and nibbled her lips as she weighed her options.

It didn't seem to make sense to give her nosy co-worker any more fuel for her wild imagination, but then there were Joel's weird actions today… Maybe Jenny would be able to give her some advice or, hopefully, tell her she was stressing over nothing. They were friends, but work friends.

So she gave Jenny the blow-by-blow of everything that had happened. Afterward, the all-knowing smirk that crossed Jenny's face made Samantha wish she had kept her mouth shut.

"Girl, he likes you and he just let you know he is in full pursuit. I love it!" Jenny smiled and gave a satisfied sigh. "Only a matter of time now before the two of you are dating."

"Dating! Girl, now I know you've lost your mind."

"Mark my words, girlfriend." Jenny kept bouncing excitedly. "Ooooo, I wonder what he's gonna do next. I have a feeling he's gonna—"

"Enough, already. It doesn't matter what he does next, because I intend to keep this relationship purely professional. The last thing I need is for my colleagues to start giving me strange looks because I started dating a patient."

"You're crazy, girlfriend. If anything, we'll all start looking at you funny if you let that fine piece of man get away. At least I know for a fact I will." Jenny started cracking up and got up from her seat.

"If you're not doing anything this weekend, stop over. Walt and the kids would love to see you, and I think we better squeeze in as many visits as possible before you start dating that fine man and no longer have time to come and visit us."

Samantha rolled her eyes.

"Walt will probably put some stuff on the grill Saturday, so stop by if you can."

"Yeah, yeah, I might stop by, but only to see the kids and Walt. But you…you with your big jinxing mouth? No way."

Jenny really cracked up then. "See you Saturday, girlfriend."

She winked and left Samantha to her contemplation.

Joel sat parked outside of the office building for Hightower Security. He had been driving past on his way home from the computer store and stopped. It was a Saturday afternoon so no one was there, but he had been inside enough times to know that the plush, modern-style offices were a far cry from the firehouse.

The firehouse had pretty much been a second home. It bustled with energy and excitement. It bristled with friendship and camaraderie. Even though Hightower Security was a family-owned business, he couldn't imagine the office building housing the same kind of vibe and pulse as the firehouse.

When he fought fires, he felt alive and worthwhile, like he was doing something important, helping people. He felt like a strong man, and even though he realized on certain levels that his masculinity wasn't wrapped up in his uniform, he still had a hard time thinking about one without the other. Where else would he be able to get that kind of feeling?

He glanced at the tall, glossy, mirrored-window

building. He didn't know if he would be able to find what he needed in there.

He thought about his discussion with his brothers a few days ago and realized it was time for him to start thinking about things he had been putting off—like what was he going to do if he could not fight fires any longer.

The probability he was done on the fire department was more than high, but he hadn't really given up hope. He held on to the belief something miraculous would happen and he would be the man he was before the accident.

It was getting harder and harder to hold on to that belief, but he couldn't let go. He didn't want to face his bleak reality. Saying he would take a position at Hightower Security felt too much like giving up. The mere thought of it caused his gut to roll and his skin to run cold.

Depression started to set in as he let out a breath and started up his vehicle. He didn't know if he would be able to survive without the thrill.

Instead of going to his parents' home and sharing a meal with them, he decided to stop by the grocery store in Elmwood Park, since it was so close to the Hightower office building in Fairlawn. They also had a wider variety of food and fresher products, and truth be told, since it was in the suburbs it was cleaner and kept up a little bit better. Plus, it wasn't too far from his town house. A bunch of TV dinners would insure he wouldn't have to be around people again until he was in a better mood.

When he got to the frozen-food aisle, he saw a sight that suddenly took all the self-pity and sad thoughts away. Instead, they were replaced with pure lust.

He saw the phenomenal backside of Samantha "Little Miss Spitfire" Dash in a pair of jean shorts and a white T-shirt tied at the side. Taking in her glossy, black, twisted hair and her luscious behind, he'd know her anywhere, from *any* angle.

She was struggling with about three bags of ice, and he rushed over to help her with them as he thought of all the amazing things he could do to her with the right amount of time and just a fraction of that ice.

He smiled as he crept up on her and relieved her of two of the bags. It was hard to remember why he had been so down just a few minutes ago. How could anyone be down when gazing at such a beautiful woman?

She gasped and turned around when he took the bags from her hands.

"See…you almost got slapped," she said with a squint of her eyes and a soft smile.

"Now that would have been a shame. You ladies want to complain chivalry is dead and yet you want to slap the first brother that goes out of his way to try and help you."

Her smile broadened. "*Whatever.* You sneaking up on a sistah is just wrong. What are you trying to do, give me a heart attack?"

"Nope. I just saw a beautiful woman who looked like she needed some help, so just hush your fuss and let me help you carry all this ice, at least something will brighten up this day." He regretted the words as soon as they came out his mouth.

After she spent so much time yesterday trying to make him feel better, the last thing he wanted to do was come off like the nickname she teased him with all the time, *Mr. Surly.*

Her beautiful brown eyes softened in concern, and he found himself wishing he could go back in time.

"What's wrong, Joel?" There was a tender lilt in her voice, the kind that could probably coax a man out of his money, time and mind.

It was so different from the tone he was used to hearing from Little Miss Spitfire. Teasing, smart aleck and opinionated were her usual fare. With this new gentle tone and expression, she seemed to really care about what was going on with him. She made his heart soften and his mouth loose.

"Nothing big. I just decided to visit the family

company today to get a feel for what my life might be like, and it was kind of…" He sighed.

No, he couldn't do this. He didn't want her pity.

She tilted her head a little as if studying him and then she nodded.

"So I take it you didn't automatically take to your possible new grazing grounds?"

Why did he ever think the spitfire would pity him? The demanding physical therapist was a taskmaster when it came to making him learn the stretching techniques and exercises for his back, and she never let him sulk or pity himself for long when in her presence. He shook his head.

"Girl, you ain't nothing nice, huh? You see a brother feeling all down and you just come in with the zingers like that dang electric stimulation you love so much. A shock a minute, huh?"

She smiled and laughed. "Come on, before my ice melts, Hightower. You don't want my pity anyway, and you're starting to love the electric stimulation now, so don't complain."

He followed her to the checkout counters and stood in line with her.

"You can just put those on the counter. I didn't mean to drag you away from your shopping. I can manage from here."

"Now what kind of gentleman would I be if I didn't

help you carry these to your car? My parents raised me better than that. Besides, I was just coming in for a couple of frozen dinners and maybe a box of Ben & Jerry's to wash away my blues."

Knowing she wasn't going to pity him was kind of freeing in a way. He could voice how pathetic he was feeling and know she was going to say something to make him snap out of it.

What would he do in a couple of weeks when his therapy sessions with her were over and he didn't have her to keep him in check?

"Aww, poor Mr. Surly, are you going to drown your sorrows in some Chunky Monkey or some Cherry Garcia? 'Cause if it's Chunky Monkey, then you and I might be able to see eye to eye on something for a change."

She had a cute little smile on her face he suddenly felt the urge to kiss off.

"Anyone with taste buds in his or her mouth knows the only flavors worth eating are Karamel Sutra and Oatmeal Cookie Crunch."

She shook her head in mock disgust. "I just don't know about you, Hightower. I just don't know."

She paid for her ice, and he helped her carry it to the car.

She stood in front of her car and gazed at him with those beautiful eyes of hers. He tried to brush off the sudden pounding in his chest and the urge to lean forward and just taste those luscious, berry-glossed lips. He tried, but he was only human. Before he could think or say a prayer that she wouldn't slap him into next week, his mouth covered hers and took over for his brain and the rest of his body.

The mouth wanted what the mouth wanted. And the way her lips automatically opened and her tongue trailed out to tangle with his told him he wasn't the only one who wanted this kiss.

He'd never tasted anything as sweet as her mouth. He groaned from deep in his gut when she pulled away.

She opened her mouth and closed it again. Before she got into her small coupe, she gave him one of those inquisitive looks, and it appeared as if she was thinking of saying something. She let out a breath and gave a half smile instead.

"I appreciate your helping me carry my packages to the car, and I guess I owe you one. Although, we may be able to say you just collected your payment... See you on Monday for your session."

He watched her get into her car and drive away, as he headed back to the frozen-food aisle he didn't even question why he was placing Ben & Jerry's Chunky Monkey in his basket along with his own favorite flavors.

After an amazing kiss like that however, he did wonder how long it was going to take him to get Samantha Dash into his home to have her ice cream. He had a couple of weeks to take care of Little Miss Spitfire, but this was one fire he wanted to let burn.

He had kissed her darn near speechless.

Samantha wanted to kick herself as she drove away from Joel. She had considered inviting him to go with her to Jenny and Walt's cookout. But then she imagined the know-it-all, I-told-you-so expression that would have crossed her friend's face, and Samantha's desire to put a smile on Mr. Surly's face was overruled by common sense.

Common sense sucked, especially when it got in the way of her spending more time with a man as fine as Joel Hightower; a man who kissed so divinely. But that was the way it had to be. If she wanted to keep her professional distance, she had to make sure she kept all desire at bay.

But the way he'd kissed her made her want to throw caution to the wind. If only he wasn't a fireman....

When she showed up at Jenny's house, she still had Joel on the brain. Trying to focus on anything else seemed impossible.

"And, so I've decided I'm leaving Walt to have a steamy ménage à trios with Denzel Washington and

Eminem, which probably won't last because I'm desperately in love with Madonna."

"That's nice," Samantha responded absently to Jenny as she replayed the way Joel's eyes seemed to soak up every inch of her body, how much she liked the way his gaze made her feel, how good his lips felt on hers.

She was in trouble.

"Now see, girl, you ain't even listening to a word I've said! What's got your attention in another world?" The irritated tone of Jenny's voice broke her reverie.

Samantha turned to her friend. "I'm listening to you. Nothing has my attention."

"Oh, really, then I guess you really do think it's a good idea for me to quit my job, take the kids and join the circus?"

"Huh?"

"And I suppose I really should buy that purple muu-muu with the matching turban and wear it to Walt's Omega Psi Phi ball?"

"Purple moo-moo? What the… No."

"Oh, but you just told me I should go on ahead and leave Walt to hook up with Denzel and Eminem even though Madonna has caught my eye."

Samantha rolled her eyes.

Okay, so maybe she hadn't been paying attention the past half hour. That didn't mean Jenny had to get all crazy.

They had finished eating and had gone inside the house to Jenny's den to chat while the kids played outside with Walt.

She loved Jenny and Walt's home on the border of Totowa and Paterson. The three-bedroom, one-and-a-half-bath home had a nice side yard with a swing and slide for the kids. Like the majority of the houses on the block, it was a Cape Cod–style house, and the inside was deceptively larger than it appeared on the outside. They had just upgraded their aluminum siding and the house was now a forest-green color that stood out among the white and yellow homes around it.

"Girl, please, you aren't even Madonna's type, and you know I got dibs on Denzel as soon as Pauletta is done with him, so you best stick with Slim Shady." Samantha laughed, and Jenny joined her after trying and failing to keep her irritated expression in tact.

"So what has your mind? Did your mom call or something?"

Samantha shook her head. "No, she didn't, and it's nothing really. You know how it is."

"Yeah, I know how it is, and the only time you'll catch me staring into space and looking all crazy eyed is when I'm thinking about my man and the loving he put on me the night before." Jenny shut her eyes for a moment as if she were having a memory, then she opened them with a teasing grin on her face. "And since we both know you don't have a man right now, and you're about to let one hell of a fine one slip away, what has your head all tripping?"

"Nada."

"Nada, my behind. Come on and 'fess up."

"Did I say nada? I meant, nonna. As in nonna yo' business…."

"Oh, I got your nonna, all right. I've fed you and you've been ignoring me for the past half hour. You gotta give me something on general principle. It's the least you can do."

"Mmm…whatever. The meals come high around here. Next time I'll stay my butt home." Samantha started laughing when she saw the sulking look on Jenny's face.

That woman knew she was nosy.

Deciding she might as well tell her friend about the grocery-store incident, Samantha spilled her guts, strategically leaving out the part about the kiss. She could just imagine how Jenny would react to that morsel of information.

"Girl! Why didn't you invite that man to come over here with you to get some food? You know you ain't right. Leaving that fine specimen to some frozen TV dinners. Plus, it would have given me an up front and personal seat to y'alls' little soap opera." Jenny actually pouted.

"It's bad enough I have to wait until Mondays, Wednesdays and Fridays to get recaps from you. The one time I could have seen the interaction for myself, you denied me."

"This is hardly about you, Jenny."

"Clearly." She pursed her lips in contemplation. "Well, I can tell you this. I don't want to have to plead and beg for any information come Monday. As soon as his appointment is over, I'm coming into your office, and I want the complete blow by blow. I can't believe you could have invited him to the cookout and didn't. You know you like the man. I don't know why you're tripping."

Samantha sighed. "What part of 'it's unprofessional to date your patients' do you not understand?"

"Oh, poo-poo to you and your professionalism. Your professionalism won't keep you warm come winter. It might be a scorching summer now, and you might think you're too hot to trot to put your heart on the line, but I bet you this winter you're gonna wish you had a man as fine as Joel Hightower to snuggle up to."

"You're so crazy, Jenny. I don't see how Walt puts up with you."

"Mark my words. If you don't give that man a

chance, you are going to regret it. You're regretting it
now. That's why you've been staring out into space
all day. You were thinking, *man, I should have invited
Joel to come with me.*"

Samantha twisted up her lips in a frown.

"Mmm, hmm—" Jenny started.

"What are you two in here scheming and plotting
about now?" Walt came into the den with Cynthia and
Walter Jr. in tow.

The youngest, Walter Jr., went immediately to his
mother's lap, and the little diva Cynthia sat down next
to Samantha on the loveseat.

The rugged rust leather sofa and loveseat worked
perfectly in their den. Samantha could just imagine
the children running and jumping on it. The worn,
rough surface of the furniture would more than likely
hide a multitude of sins.

Samantha absolutely adored Jenny and Walt's children. They were two of the most well-behaved kids
she'd ever seen and they looked like miniature versions of Jenny and Walt.

"We're not scheming and plotting. I'm trying to get
Miss Meany here to stop giving this really nice man
a hard time."

Samantha laughed. It was funny how Joel suddenly
went from Mr. Super Fine to a really nice man when
Jenny's husband was around.

"That's all you pretty women do is give a brother a hard time. Look at how hard I had to work to get you to give me a second look. I'm surprised you're giving out advice on how not to play hard to get." Walt sat down on the sofa next to Jenny and put his arm around her, pulling her and Walt Jr. close.

The love so clearly evident on his face for his wife and children nearly took Samantha's breath away. Walt was looking at Jenny in a way that clearly said, if they didn't have company and these kids were fast asleep, he'd have her climbing the walls.

Samantha wondered when she would get a man to look at her like that.

Joel Hightower's handsome brown face and daring brown eyes popped into her head at that moment, and she realized a man had looked at her exactly the way Walt now looked at Jenny. Only, she had no idea what she was going to do about it.

"Stop fooling around, Walt. You know I didn't give you a hard time." Jenny leaned into her husband's arms and smiled coyly.

"Hmm. Somebody is creating a little revisionist history. You had me chasing you around campus our entire freshman year before you even let a brother carry your books." Walt turned to Samantha with a big grin on his face. "Don't let this woman give you advice. She almost let a good catch like me get away."

"Mmm. Mmm, hmm. Modest, isn't he?" Jenny laughed. "With that ego, it's a wonder I didn't have him wait two years."

"See, she admits it." Walt placed a kiss on Jenny's cheek.

"There's nothing wrong with making a man work for your attentions, but she's not doing that. She's seriously thinking about not giving him a chance at all. Talking about being all professional." Jenny frowned.

"I thought we came inside for dessert?" Cynthia let out an exasperated sigh.

"Yeah, I want a sundae." Walt Jr. started bouncing up and down on Jenny's lap, and Samantha could tell the little impatient boy must take after Jenny.

Walt stood up and shuttled the children toward the kitchen. He turned before leaving. "Remember what I said, Jenny is the *last* person that should be dishing out advice."

He started laughing and ducked when Jenny sent a throw pillow sailing toward his head.

Samantha twisted her lips to the side.

Jenny placed her hand on her hip. "What? Girl, please. If anything, that makes me the perfect person to give advice on the subject. You don't want to waste a year of good loving with a fine man like I did. You already wasted over two months."

"Whatever. If it were meant to be, he wouldn't be

a patient. The fates would have had us meet in a work-free zone under completely different circumstances."

"Just promise me this. If he makes a move, you won't shoot him down. Take a minute to get to know the man at least, as a friend. We could all use good friends."

Samantha let the idea circle around in her head. Jenny's suggestion seemed pretty harmless and useful, but there was only one problem. Could she really be friends with Joel Hightower and not want more? Could she be friends after feeling what it was like to kiss him?

After sharing that intense kiss with Samantha, Joel felt too hyped to stay home and sulk, so he decided to visit his younger brother, Jason, and his wife, Penny. Their town house was located in West Paterson near Garret Mountain. The gray-and-white stone buildings that made up the complex appeared to have been recently built and had a very modern design. It wasn't too far from his town house in Passaic Park, so he dropped off his frozen dinners and gave his brother a call.

Jason had been about to put some steaks on the grill and seemed more than happy to throw one more on for Joel.

Penny greeted Joel with such a warm and welcoming hug, he knew without a doubt he'd made the right decision to hang out with them.

"I'm so glad you decided to stop by. We don't see you enough." Penny led him out to the deck where Jason was grilling.

"What's up, bro? It's good to see you," Jason greeted him with a playful grin as they hugged and gave each other pounds.

"Would you like a beer or a glass of wine? Soda? Water?" Penny stopped before sitting down on the lounge chair that had a copy of *Vibe Vixen* laying flat on it.

"I'll take a beer, if you don't mind." Joel took a seat in the teakwood patio chair next to the chair he assumed Penny had been sitting in.

She went back inside to get the beer, and Jason seemed fixated on her walk.

"Look at you, all in love. And to think, you have me to thank for all this happiness you're experiencing." Joel had to pat himself on the back for giving his brother the good advice to forgive the woman he loved.

"If I remember correctly, you laughed at me for a good long time before you gave up the advice." Jason turned the steaks and then took a seat across from him.

"I had to give you a hard time first, but I did give you good advice."

"Yes, you did. But I'd like to think I would have

come to the right decision anyway, after a while."
Jason chuckled. "I'll tell you what, when you need
some good advice, feel free to call on me."

"Who's dishing out advice?" Penny came back
outside and handed Joel a beer. "You know, I give advice for a living as a consultant and stylist. I'd be
happy to tell you two what to do, and I won't even
charge you my going rate."

"Oh, that's okay, sis. You'll have your hands full
with my baby bro." Joel took a sip from his beer as
he chuckled.

Jason leaned over and gave Penny a peck on the
lips, and she caressed his face gently. The loving expressions on their faces filled Joel with longing.

For the first time since his accident, he wanted something besides a strong enough back to return to the job
that thrilled him and made him feel like a man. He
wanted someone to look at him the way Penny looked
at his brother, and he wanted to gaze at someone in the
special way his brother was gazing at Penny.

He thought of Samantha's soft, inquisitive expression a few hours ago in the grocery-store parking lot.
He thought of their kiss. He realized he liked her a lot
and he wondered... She was already the woman
working to give him one thing he wanted. He wondered if she could be the woman to give him all the
things he now knew he needed.

That night he dreamed, and for the first time in a long time he woke up in the cold sweat of desire. A certain sassy-mouthed physical therapist had waltzed into his dreams and took him to heights he wasn't sure he'd be able to reach again in real life, but he knew the invigorated feeling gave him a new purpose. He had to find out if the sexy siren from his dreams could be the woman to give him all the things he now knew he wanted.

Chapter 6

Samantha eyed Joel suspiciously. From the moment she'd walked into the room and started his treatments, he had been chipper and pleasant. Even when she showed him new stretching exercises to help deal with and manage his back pain, he kept his incredibly disarming smile on his face. He hadn't made one grumpy grunt or wisecrack. By the time they made it to her office for the consultation, she was flustered beyond belief. She'd foolishly tried to convince herself that the kiss was just a fluke and they could go on as if it had never happened.

Yeah, right.

And Joel's sparkling and very devilish stare didn't help in the least. She took a deep breath and leaned back in her chair.

He smiled again, and all she could see was trouble. Why should she care if he smiled at her? He was a patient and that was it. A patient full of devilishness and trouble.

"Okay, Hightower, what gives?"

He frowned. "What do you mean?"

"I mean, why are you being all nice and agreeable? What kind of plot do you have working in that head of yours? You're not planning on trying to kiss me again, are you?"

He laughed, and the rich sound echoed through her soul. In the two-and-a-half months she had been treating him, she didn't think she had ever heard him laugh like that. It was the same full-bodied, hearty laugh she remembered from the news report after his accident. *Trouble.*

"I like you. What are you doing for lunch tomorrow?"

"Eating."

"How about we eat together? I normally have lunch a couple of times a week at the best hot-dog spot in town. But I'm willing to forgo my favorite to take you out to a really nice restaurant and get to know you better, outside of this clinic."

She nearly swallowed her tongue.

Pursing her lips, she studied him carefully. She noticed his eyes zero in on her lips just before his tongue licked his own lips LL Cool J-style. And it didn't get sexier than that.

She shook her head. Even if he was attracted to her, they couldn't pursue anything. He was a patient. She did not work her way through undergraduate school and two graduate degrees to throw it all away by having an affair with a patient, and there was also the fact that he was about to go back to a dangerous job. No. She couldn't give in.

"Well, as much as I love Willy's Taste of the Chi's hot dogs, I'm afraid not even the possibility of having one of those could make me go out on a date with a patient."

He frowned, and if she hadn't become so attached to the sweet and sexy way his happy face appeared, she might have relished the return of his normal demeanor.

"Willy's what? The best hot dogs in the area are located at Johnny's Grill. They make the best Texas-style wieners this side of Jersey."

"Texas-style, hmm… Yeah… I think *not.* You really haven't lived until you've tasted a Chicago-style hot dog."

"Chicago-style. Chicago can't even get pizza right. What do they know about hot dogs?"

"Excuse you? Chicago-style pizza is the only way

to really eat pizza. The deep dish makes it a meal. That thin stuff y'all eat around here leaves a lot to be desired."

He started laughing and shaking his head. "Girl, it's a good thing I'm here to help you see the error of your ways and put your taste buds on the right path. I'll have to break my date rules and forgo the fancy restaurants for now so you can get a taste of a real hot dog and then some real pizza. But clearly the desperate state of this situation calls for a change in plans."

"Change in plans? Date? Did you say *date?* Listen, Joel, you're my patient, and I realize you may have formed an attachment to me because of the nature of our relationship, but that will pass—"

"I don't want it to pass. I want to explore it. I feel more alive around you than I've felt in months. All I know is you owe me one for the help I gave you at the supermarket, and the least you can do is let me treat you to a hot dog so I can prove to you Johnny's Grill is far superior to Willy's whatever."

She folded her arms across her chest, prepared to argue him down and tell him that, in addition to it being unprofessional, she wasn't going to go out to lunch with him because there was no way a Texas wiener could best a Chi-town dog, but then she saw the way he was leaning there with his sexy smile. She would never get tired of seeing it, along with the confidence she suddenly decided he wore really well, even when he was so sure he would have her.

And she knew it then, just by looking at the gleam in his beautiful brown eyes that spelled trouble. He meant to have her, and at that moment, she knew she wanted exactly what he wanted.

So when her mouth opened, instead of the wise-crack or gentle letdown she knew she should give, something entirely inappropriate fell out of her mouth.

"How about I meet you at this Johnny's Grill for dinner tonight and we have lunch at Willy's tomorrow? That way, at least you get a good lunch out of the deal when I rub your face in the fact Chicago-style hot dogs reign supreme."

"That sounds fabulous to me, except for the part about you meeting me there. I told you, my parents raised an honorable gentleman. I have to pick you up for the date, Samantha."

"This is not a date, Joel."

"Call it what you want, sweetheart, but I'll be driving you to Johnny's. So am I your last appointment for the day? Should I follow you home to drop off your car and then we can hit up the spot? Or would you like to give me your address and I'll swing by your place in about an hour or so? Oh, and to answer your earlier question… I do plan on kissing you again, and again, and again…."

Samantha couldn't stop her traitorous lips from smiling. There didn't seem to be any turning back now, and she certainly didn't want to turn back. So she gave the devilish Mr. Hightower her address and tried to still the rapid beating of her heart.

Sitting across from Samantha in his favorite diner, Joel almost couldn't believe it. If he'd known this was even possible, he wouldn't have wasted the first two-and-a-half months of his therapy being a grouch. He should have started pursuing her from the moment he laid eyes on her. Now he had to make up for lost time.

She took another tentative bite of her hot dog and rolled her eyes as she chewed.

He watched her lean back in her chair, cross her legs and then cross her arms over her chest. He wouldn't have been surprised to find her little fingers crossed, as well, because he was sure she was about to tell a fib and say Johnny's Texas-style wieners weren't as good as the Chicago-style she loved.

The woman would do *anything* not to agree with him.

She pursed her lips a second and then frowned. "Well, if you deep-fry anything and slap some sauce on it, it's bound to have some flavor."

"Yes, but are they *good?*"

"Didn't I just say that? Deep-fried food is good."

"Yes, but are these hot dogs the best you've ever had? Are they better than your Willy's Chi-town dogs?"

"You're not gonna get me to say that. No self-respecting girl from the Chi is going to admit to something like that. I'll just say they were good, and we can leave it at that." She smiled that sexy half smile, half smirk of hers and started eating her hot dog and fries with gravy.

Figuring that was about the most he would get her to admit to, he polished off the rest of his meal and then leaned back. He liked a woman who wasn't afraid to enjoy her food and wasn't constantly on a diet. He could count on one hand the number of women he'd ever dated who would even consider eating one of the deep-fried hot dogs covered in chili sauce, mustard and onions, let alone have the fries and root beer with it. Samantha Dash was definitely a woman he could see himself falling for.

Who was he kidding? He had already started falling. The trick was getting her to fall right along with him.

"What're you looking at?" She tilted her head to the side as she studied him.

"You."

"Why?"

"I was just trying to figure out how I'm going to make you as crazy about me as I'm becoming about you."

He wondered what would happen when he kissed

her again, because he fully intended to kiss her again. Would she still have that stunned expression on her face? He planned to find out tonight, because those lips had been calling him ever since he tasted them in the parking lot, and it was high time he answered.

"Nothing can happen between us, Joel. You're my patient. Have you ever thought maybe you've developed this attraction to me because you see me as some sort of savior? You know, given my role in your recovery—"

He had to laugh at that. "Sweetheart, while I do believe you are the best at what you do and I'm so grateful I have you on my recovery team, I know the difference. You don't see me having erotic dreams starring Dr. Lardner, do you? He performed the operations that made it possible for me to even be in physical therapy with you."

She sucked her teeth. "*Ha. Ha.* You know what I mean, Joel. And…erotic dreams? You've been having erotic dreams about me?"

Nodding, he leaned forward and reached across the table, taking her hand in his. "And not of the savior-complex variety.…"

As soon as he touched her hand, a shock went through him and his pulse quickened. He hadn't felt that kind of thrill in so long. The excitement of the moment was almost overwhelming.

"Joel, it's unprofessional—"

"Tell me you're not attracted to me. Say it, and I'll leave you alone." He gritted his teeth after speaking the words.

What if she said it? He knew he wouldn't be able to leave her alone. *Hell no.* He wanted her.

Silent, she sucked her bottom lip into her mouth.

He felt a shock to his groin. He wanted that lip. He wanted her lips on his.

"I think we should leave now."

At least she didn't say she wasn't attracted to him. Should he force the issue and make her answer?

No. Give it time.

Keeping her hand in his, he rose and they walked out of Johnny's Grill, hand in hand.

His touch gave her goose bumps in the middle of summer. The tingling feeling covering her skin and coursing through her body was *not* a good sign.

It was a good feeling, however… Dear God, it felt good, but not a good sign at all.

Her body's reaction to just the simple touch of his hand, to just walking with him holding her hand felt like what the gentle shock of the electric stimulation patches she worked with would feel like if you were riding a roller coaster at the same time.

She stepped into his large SUV as he held the door

open for her and smiled softly when he closed it after her. The thudding of her heart would have worried her if she hadn't had a checkup recently and received a clean bill of health. Heart palpitations like the ones Joel Hightower caused could make a sister think she was having a heart attack.

But then she was under attack, wasn't she?

As he got into the SUV and started it up, he looked at her with those devilish brown eyes, those sexy drops of seduction, and she knew everything Jenny had said was true.

What was she going to do about the fact Joel Hightower was on the prowl and had her in his sights?

"So I'll pick you up at around 12:30 p.m. tomorrow?"

"Pick me up? For what?"

"Lunch. Remember, we have to have your little Chicago-style hot dogs, unless you want to forfeit now? That won't get you out of lunch, though. It'll just get you a better meal at a fancy restaurant."

She'd forgotten she had made the challenge back at the office. What in the world had she been thinking? She must have been out of her mind.

However, she wasn't a punk, and she wasn't about to back down. Those little Texas-style wieners were cute and all, but they certainly didn't hold a candle to an authentic Chicago-style hot dog.

"I'll meet you at Willy's, Joel. I can't have you picking me up from the clinic. It wouldn't look—"

"Professional." He rolled his eyes as he cut her off and finished her statement. "You're going to have to get over that, Little Miss Spitfire. Because I mean to make you mine, and I couldn't care less about how we met or any of that. And at some point, I will be picking you up from your job to take you to lunch, dinner, who knows? I might even feel the urge to send flowers, just because. And I don't do the secret relationship thing."

"Relationship? Slow your roll, brother. Don't you think you're moving a tad too fast here? I mean, really, we just had one meal together and—"

"We had two-and-a-half months of chemistry and undeniable sexual tension. One amazing kiss… And I'm tired of ignoring what I'm feeling. We've had a simmering seduction that has teetered just on the edge of heating through. And now, sweetheart…now we're going to make it hot."

Stunned, she gulped, and her chest thumped so loudly it echoed in her ears.

He leaned over.

How come she didn't even notice they had stopped in front of her apartment complex? Because she was too busy trying to resist the sweet lull of his baritone voice.

And why was she just sitting there looking at him with her mouth open when he was leaning so close, *so close?*

Aah…

His lips were soft.

They were just as soft as she remembered them.

His tongue darted in and out of her mouth slowly, and the pressure of his lips caused a subtle moan to escape from deep in her gut.

She allowed her tongue to meet his, and they wrapped around one another in a tantalizing dance, each trying to wind around to the top over and over again. She let him land on top and then she pulled her tongue away to trace his lips.

A groan came from him that made her imagine what it would be like to hear that sound while she was wrapped in his arms. It would sound so good. She knew it would.

He pulled away. "Let me walk you to your door."

"You don't have to. I—"

His slanted his right eye and he frowned. "Didn't I tell you how I was raised, woman? I'll walk you to your door."

It didn't make sense to argue with him. He was going to do it anyway.

She got out of the truck and waited for him to come around.

"You're going to make it hard for me to show you what a gentleman I can be, aren't you?" He took her hand in his, and they walked to her door.

She always forgot stuff like letting the guy open the door for her. As far as she was concerned, she could open her own doors, but a guy like Joel Hightower just might make her think about waiting until he came around and opened the door. He made chivalry seem a little less archaic and more…sexy.

And she had to admit she liked the way his gentleman skills worked with his wooing.

Standing in front of the door to her apartment, she was torn between inviting him in for a nightcap and running as fast as her legs could carry her away from temptation. When he stepped forward and placed those lips of his on hers, she felt the tingling again from the flesh of her mouth to the tops of her toes. His arms caressed her shoulders, and he used his hold to pull her body flush with his. His hands traveled down her back and teasingly gripped her bottom.

Between the door at her back and the hard muscled strength in front of her, she realized being caught never felt so good. Allowing her hands to explore his massive, masculine chest, she could feel the tingles explode from her fingertips with each touch.

He suckled on her lips as if he could get a life-sustaining liquid from them. She savored the pull of his mouth on hers. It felt like more than a kiss. It felt as if her soul was somehow escaping her body and his was entering hers, and it made her so aroused she knew she had to end the kiss and make a mad dash into her apartment while she was still thinking sanely.

Even though he seemed to be ready and willing to make it hot and take their relationship up a few hundred degrees, she needed a little more time. At least her mind needed more time even if her body seemed to be screaming, *Yes, take me now.*

She pulled away, and he groaned.

"I better get inside now. I'll meet you at Willy's tomorrow at twelve-thirty. It's over on Church Street in Paterson."

He nodded. "I'll see you there, and be ready to eat a little humble pie for dessert, because you and your little Chicago dogs are going down."

Laughing, she opened the door. "Whatever. I just hope those deep-fried death dogs you had me eating tonight don't give me indigestion."

She heard his hearty laughter as she closed her door. She was already knee-deep in the heat, and she didn't think she would get out of it if she could.

Chapter 7

It was a bad-back day, a bad-back day and Joel was stuck in his town house with his mother, Celia Hightower, and his aunt Sophie each running around trying to outdo one another being "helpful."

He was stuck with his mother and aunt instead of out having lunch with Little Miss Spitfire. *Grouchy* and *irritable* didn't even begin to cover his funk.

As Celia and Aunt Sophie each reached for and struggled with his pillow to fluff it at the same time, he felt his slowly boiling blood bubble over. Celia let go of the pillow and Sophie tumbled back, barely catching herself from hitting the hardwood floor. A small barely noticeable smirk crossed Celia's face and quickly disappeared, but not soon enough for Sophie to miss it. Sophie pursed her lips and arched her broad shoulders. She fluffed the pillow and placed it back on the bed.

Enough was enough.

No matter how much pain he was in today, seeing his mother duke it out with her sister-in-law and long-time rival wasn't going to help him feel better. They seemed to be getting worse and worse as the years went by.

"You know, Mom, Aunt Sophie, I really appreciate that you both rushed on over here when you found out I was having some pain, but I think I'll be okay on my own."

"Nonsense. You need some help, and luckily your auntie is a retired nurse," Sophie said as she glared at Celia.

Celia's lips twitched.

"Sometimes nothing is better than a little TLC from your mother," Celia assured.

"All the mothering in the world can't beat a trained health-care professional," Sophie offered with a twist of her lips.

"Spoken like someone who never had any children of her own." Celia's words faltered off into a soft little chuckle.

Sophie's back arched, and her teeth clamped tightly as she smiled. "It's a good thing I didn't have a family of my own. My little brother needed me to help make sure his boys were raised *properly.*"

"Hmm…" Celia pursed her lips in mock contemplation. "Is that how they're describing *meddling* these days?"

"All right, ladies. I can see this is about to get ugly. Clearly, you both can't stay."

And it would get even uglier if he finished what he wanted to say.

"I'm not leaving. You're my son. You're in pain." His mother stopped and glared at Sophie. "I can normally let things slide. You know I rarely let folks get me riled up. But when it comes to my children and their wellness, I'm not letting anything or *anyone* get in the way."

"If you care so much, as a *mother,* then you should want me to stay. I'm the trained professional. You have no health-care training."

"I'm his mother."

Joel shook his head. "I'm getting a little tired. Can y'all take this discussion into the living room? I need a nap."

They weren't going to leave. He couldn't make them, and he didn't have the energy to try. Plus, he would much rather spend his time thinking about how he was going to get Samantha to consider rescheduling their lunch date.

She sounded cool on the phone when he called to cancel, but as he remembered how hard it was to get her to agree in the first place, he couldn't help but curse his aching back. Sure, it was the reason he even met his spunky temptress in the first place, but it was certainly getting in the way of his plans to woo her.

"Fine, son. I'll be downstairs, tidying up," Celia said after giving him a peck on the forehead.

"And I'll see what you have in the fridge and make lunch and maybe some dinner—" Sophie started.

"No!" He realized how harsh and immediate his response to Aunt Sophie's offer to cook was, too late to stop himself.

Aunt Sophie had to be the worst cook in the family. She was always trying to make dishes to outdo his mother, but Sophie couldn't touch Celia in the kitchen.

"What I mean is, I don't want you two doing any work. Mom, if you clean up, I'll never find half my things. You know you have a habit of throwing things away. And, Aunt Sophie, I have enough food and leftovers to last me a lifetime. You guys have set me up fine in that regard. You don't have to cook anymore. So if both you ladies are staying, just watch TV in the den or something."

If he was forced to eat Sophie's cooking, he would

have to leap from his second-floor bedroom window, bad back or not.

A knowing smile crossed Celia's face. "Fine. I won't touch your things, but I'll be here if you need me."

The two women left the room, and he leaned back against the pillow in exasperation.

Getting through the day and not being in a bad mood had been a chore.

She should have been more than a little relieved she didn't go on a second "date," for lack of a better word, with Joel. She had dodged a bullet in a real way. She should be grateful the fates had intervened.

But all she had been able to think about was his slow, sexy smile; brown bedroom eyes; and how easy they were able to talk to and confide in one another. She couldn't get rid of the fact she had been looking forward to talking with him again and finding out more about him.

Fine, smart, seductive brothers did not show up every day in a woman's life. He epitomized everything she ever wanted in a man, except for the fact he was a patient. And he held a dangerous job.

So why in heaven's name did she find herself ringing his doorbell when she got off from work?

She was a physical therapist, not a country family doctor who made house calls, but there she was....

She almost turned and walked away after ringing the bell.

"Yes?" a sweet soft voice that Samantha assumed was his mother's greeted her from the door.

Turning back around, she smiled. There was no way the women would remember her from the hospital all those months ago, after Joel had his accident. The biggest concern would be coming up with a plausible reason why his physical therapist was making house calls.

"I'm Samantha, Joel's physical therapist."

"You're his physical therapist? Little Miss Spitfire, the taskmaster?" She smiled.

"I can't believe Mr. Surly's running around telling folks his little nickname for me." The words slipped out before she thought about the fact she was standing in front of his mom.

His mother gave her one of those looks that people got when they thought they had things all figured out, as if she was putting two and two together in her head and coming up with God knows what.

"Anyway," she tried to cover, "maybe I should go, since he has you here to check up on him... I was just stopping by because he...ah...called earlier, and I just wanted to—"

"Oh, don't leave. You can't leave now. Now that I see who his physical therapist is, there's no way I can

let you leave, my darling girl. Even when he's complaining about how difficult a session was and how
you never cut him any slack, he does it with a smile."
Mrs. Hightower opened the door wider and waved her
in.

Samantha walked in, and it felt as if she were
walking the plank. Besides, a soulfully sexy man with
back pain and his sweet mother, she had no idea what
else awaited her inside the town house.

"This is actually perfect. I'm glad you stopped by.
I was going to go looking for my son's therapist anyway." Mrs. Hightower winked at her. "I wanted to
check you out and see what has Joel in a better mood
these days."

The older woman patted Samantha's back as she
led her into the house. "Well, he's nowhere near his
usual playful and funny self, but he's much better
than he was a few months ago. And now that I see you,
I can see why."

"What do you mean? I'm just his therapist."

"Nonsense. His eyes light up when he talks about
you." Mrs. Hightower just kept walking and talking,
and Samantha just followed against her better judgment.

All this talk had her heart doing flip-flops it had
no business doing. It didn't matter what his eyes did
when he talked about her. It didn't matter how her

body heated up when she thought about him or how her emotions started short-circuiting when he smiled or made one of his innuendos and it certainly didn't matter how her blood burned and her knees buckled from his kisses, because she had no business kissing him.

"Who is *she?*" Another larger woman with big shoulders and even bigger breasts blocked the stairway into the next room like a linebacker.

"This is Joel's physical therapist. She's here to check up on him, and I'm sure he'll be glad to see her." His mother grabbed Samantha's hand and led her around the linebacker and up the stairs.

The linebacker followed them up the steps. "Since when do physical therapists make house calls this hour of the evening? Something doesn't seem quite right about this, Celia, but I guess nobody can tell you anything. You'd just let any ole thing in the house talking about she's a physical therapist."

Samantha put her hand on her hip and stopped. She counted to ten and reminded herself that she was visiting Joel's house for the first time and it wouldn't be proper to let her South Side of Chicago girl come out.

Joel's mother sucked her teeth and kept walking. "I know she's a physical therapist, Sophie, because now I remember seeing her a lot in the hospital when Joel had the accident."

"And she just conveniently ended up his therapist? Sounds like she could be some kind of stalker to me."

"Oh, Sophie, hush. This woman is no more a stalker than you or I, and I think seeing her will cheer my grumpy son up."

Samantha's stomach started to flutter and she reached out to hold on to the railing as she followed Celia up the stairs.

Celia knocked on Joel's door and turned to beam her bright, happy smile at Samantha.

Samantha managed a weak smile back. She could hear Sophie suck her teeth directly behind her. The woman seemed to be so close Samantha swore she felt a hiss of air sweep past her neck.

"Yeah?" Joel's masculine voice called from behind the door.

"Son, you have company. Can we come in?"

The was a slight pause and then a hesitant, "Yeah."

Celia turned and smiled again before opening the door.

Samantha didn't follow her directly in and regretted it when Sophie stepped on the back of her heel.

"Move it along, girl," Sophie snapped in an agitated tone.

No. She. Didn't. She didn't even apologize or say excuse me or anything! This old woman is really asking for a good ole Chi-town cuss out.

Samantha walked into the bedroom and caught Joel's eyes.

His eyes widened and gleamed. His full, luscious lips took on a sweet, seductive smile. His entire aura seemed to glow.

"So you couldn't stay away from me, huh?" he said with a sexy grin.

She blinked and swallowed. "When you said on the phone how much pain you were in, I thought I'd help."

"Well, I've seen all I need to see. I'll be downstairs, Joel. Be sure to invite this lovely young woman to the family cookout next Saturday. I like this one." Celia's voice seemed to sing.

"Mmmph." Sophie rolled her eyes. "Celia, sometimes I really don't think you have the sense God gave a flea."

"Let's go, Sophie, and leave these young people alone. I'm sure she's going to help him with his back and whip him right into shape." Celia took a hold of Sophie's arm and led her out of the room.

When the door closed, Samantha sat on the edge of the bed.

"Did you even try to do any of the stretching exercises when you felt the discomfort starting?"

"Come here."

"What? Boy, I'm here. I'm trying to—"

"Come here. Come closer to me."

She got up and went to the head of the bed where he sat up with a bunch of pillows behind his back.

He reached up and caressed her cheek.

"You know, if you use the pain-management techniques I showed you, you'll find that you can—"

He leaned forward and covered her mouth with his.

His tongue felt so warm and strong. As he forged into her mouth, she couldn't help but surrender to his caress. He licked, nipped and nibbled, making her mouth his feasting ground, but his tasting had nothing on her hunger. She found her teeth all too ready to devour as she took a hold of his lips and suckled.

He lifted her shirt and massaged her breasts. The gentle kneading motions of his hands caused her breath to hitch. When his fingers found her nipples, she was forced to wonder how in the world she ever survived without his touch. She leaned closer and closer to him as shock waves coursed through her body.

"I knew it! She's no physical therapist. Must be some kind of call girl!" Sophie's shrill, accusing voice stopped their tongue and body exploration cold.

They both turned to the door and found her standing there, pointing her finger and them with a horrified expression on her face.

Joel let out a sigh. "Aunt Sophie, thank you for coming by today to help out, but you can go home now. Tell Mom she can go home, too."

"But—"

"Honestly, Aunt Sophie, you guys can leave now. I'm feeling better."

"Mmmph. I bet you are." Sophie's shoulders reared up, and she turned to leave, slamming the door behind her.

"Come back here." The words were spoken in a low, sexy, commanding voice that caused goose bumps to pop up all over her arms.

"Joel, this is not right. Your aunt has a point. As your physical therapist I have no business in your bedroom, on your bed, kissing you." She sighed.

It was so hard to do the right thing after being kissed almost senseless. Good thing Sophie barged in. Who knows what might have happened if the old, evil woman hadn't?

A series of bad-back-friendly sexual positions ran through her head.

Oh, God. She should not be thinking about any of that.

He grinned and leaned back on the pillows, licking his lips as if he was still trying to taste her.

"Talk to me. Tell me about yourself. I wanna learn everything I can about you. Did you always want to be a physical therapist? Do you have any brothers and sisters? You've told me about your dad. What about your mom? Is she still in Chicago?"

She cleared her throat. Talking about her warped family life was the last thing she wanted to do. "You have plenty of time later to learn all there is to know about me. Right now we need to do something about that back pain."

She shot up from the bed.

"Get up, Hightower. I'm going to have you do some minimal stretching and then I'm going to give you a deep-tissue massage and then I'm going home."

"But I feel better already. As soon as I saw your face, I felt ten times better."

She couldn't contain her chuckle. "And just imagine how much better you'll feel once I put you through your paces?"

He groaned, but he slowly got up from the bed. She vowed to help him and then get out of there, before she slipped up and made sweet love to the most intoxicating man she'd ever known.

Joel couldn't believe he had had Samantha in his home and had only managed to get a couple of kisses. At least his back wasn't bothering him as much and he would be able to keep his appointment with her tomorrow. He wouldn't miss that for anything in the world. He planned to get her to open up and trust him. He had no idea what was holding her back, but he knew he wouldn't stop until he broke down all her barriers.

Whether Samantha was willing to admit it or not, she was feeling him. It was time to turn the heat up from sizzling to scorching. The summer was about to get hot, and it had nothing to do with the weather.

Samantha entered her apartment and fell out on her bed. How did she manage to leave Joel Hightower's place without tasting his delicious, full lips again and running her own lips up and down his hard, taut, muscular body? She floated on her memories of their kisses until she noticed her message light blinking on her phone and pressed to see who called. She would have put money on it being Jenny with her nosy behind.

"Sammie, I was looking through the paper the other day, and I saw they have several physical therapist jobs here in Chicago—"

She skipped the message. Even though her mother sounded pretty sober. She still didn't feel like listening to the why-don't-you-get-a-job-here routine.

"Sammie…baby…where are you?" There was a sob and a hiccup. "You know you could come home. I need you. Why won't you come home?"

Samantha deleted the message.

She had figured out early on how to tiptoe around her mother's feelings and moods. The first time her mother lashed out at her in a drunken tirade a few months after her father died, it was because she was missing her daddy and tried to talk to her mother about it. The way Veronica had cursed her out that evening was nothing compared to the glass that barely missed her head. She still got the shakes when she thought about her mother's reaction to her throwing out all of the alcohol in the house during her freshman year in high school.

Samantha let the next message play.

"You're just one selfish, ungrateful little bitch. That's what you are, after all I've done for you. You could at least bring your little ass home—"

Delete.

She couldn't take hearing any more of her mother's hateful, ugly words. Samantha let out a gush of pent-up energy in the form of a sob.

One day she would have to deal with her mother. *But not today....*

She collapsed onto her sofa and stopped trying to block out her memories. She let out deep, long, mournful sobs, and each one reminded her why she could never let herself fall in love with a man who had a dangerous job, a man who could one day leave another gaping hole in her heart. Too bad she had a feeling it was already too late to stop the falling in love part. She only hoped it didn't end up as badly for her as it had for her mother.

Chapter 8

Joel felt much better the next day. The doctors had been right. There really was no rhyme or reason to the flare-ups. He did know he would be sure to do those stretching techniques Samantha taught him to try and stay on top of things. Being stuck in bed with pain was not ideal.

Not when he finally found someone he wanted to get out of bed for and share his bed with.

With the pain gone for now, he really had no excuse to keep putting off thinking about his possible new life, so he went to visit Hightower Security again. Maybe this time he'd actually go inside.

His father had invested well and had been able to retire early and start his own business. The investments, the company, the Hightower home that had been in the family for generations and Celia Hightower's former position in the upper administration of the Paterson School district as the assistant superintendent meant that the family never really fit the typical blue-collar cops and firemen mold. Once Hightower Security really started to take off, they all became accustomed to a level of comfort that most folks dream of.

When he entered his father's office, James Hightower seemed happy to see him. The two of them hugged and shook hands before they settled down.

"I'm glad you're here, son. I know you didn't envision yourself working here so soon, but I have to say, if it turns out you can't return to the fire department, I'd appreciate it if you gave it a shot."

"I know, Dad. That's the only thing that makes the possibility that I'll have to leave my career halfway bearable, knowing that you've been wanting one or all of us to be more involved with the company for the longest time." He cracked a smile he wasn't feeling.

"Yes. Don't get me wrong. I love our family's legacy, and I love that my sons are continuing the legacy…" Pausing for dramatic effect, he continued, "Even those of you who went the fireman route." The former police officer laughed.

The friendly rivalry between the cops and firemen in his family would never die. Even though the older Hightower was no longer in his job, and there was a small chance that the younger one may never be able to return to his job, when it came to the Hightower legacy and the ongoing battle, they picked sides and still held their roles.

However, Joel didn't feel like playing out the old verbal fireman versus cops today.

James Hightower must have noticed the change in his son's mood because he sobered rather quickly.

"You know I started the company because I saw what my job was doing to your mother. She put on a brave front for years, and she still does with all of her sons—her babies—in dangerous jobs. It was hard for her not knowing if her man was going to come home."

"But, Dad, tomorrow isn't promised to anyone, no matter what kind of job they have, and if you have to die, dying trying to do good and save lives is the way to go."

"I know, but for me, after years on the force and years of seeing the fear in my wife's eyes I decided to start another family legacy, an optional one, still in the business of protection, but a little bit safer." James shuddered. "And after holding and comforting my wife when she thought she was going lose you… I'm glad I started the company. I never want to see my wife cry like that again. I can't take it. If she would have lost you—if we had lost you—it would have broken her heart, and her heart is my heart." Choked up, James shook his head, remembering the night of the accident.

Joel nodded. What could he say to that? Besides, if his father hadn't started Hightower Security, then Joel really would be stuck.

And Joel couldn't take his mother's tears any more than his father could. That's why he didn't complain too much when she came over to help out and ended up hovering. It was her way of dealing with her emotions. He got that.

His father patted him on the back. "So, I'd be glad to have you here, son, really glad. With you here, maybe I'd be able to retire earlier and spend some time with your mother."

Panic set in. "Now hold on, Dad. Don't try and leave me here just yet. Even if I didn't go back to fighting fires and joined the company, I would still have a lot to learn."

"Don't worry, I'd give you a little time to get the lay of the land. But trust me, when you find a woman you love as much as I love your mother, you'll be looking forward to uninterrupted time with her."

He thought of Samantha's smiling face and the

jokes she always used to keep him grounded. He certainly wanted to spend time with her away from everything and everyone.

"I think I know what you mean, Dad." He couldn't stop the big old grin that came across his face, and he realized he didn't want to.

His father folded his arms across his chest and studied Joel carefully.

"Now that's an expression I don't think I've ever seen on your face before, son."

"What expression? A smile. You've seen me smile before. Maybe not a lot lately, but—"

"No, not the smile. Although, it is good to see you smiling again, damn good. I'm talking about that Hightower-in-love look." James started chuckling. "Who is she? Do we know her?"

Sure he was attracted to Samantha. What red-blooded man wouldn't be?

But in love?

His father must be seeing things.

James just continued chuckling over Joel's puzzled face.

"Must be still new, because you're acting like you don't have a clue. Don't worry, you'll know any day now. The love bug will hit you smack, dab in the middle of the eyes. The reason I know the look is because I see it every day in the mirror, or when I think about your mother, and recently whenever I look at my youngest son with his new bride."

No way was his father saying he was walking around here looking all giddy and ga-ga like Jason. His younger brother was on constant grin and crazy in love.

"I think you're seeing things, Dad. I'm interested in a woman—my physical therapist to be exact. But it's way too soon to start calling what I'm feeling *love*. I'm interested and I'm in pursuit, yes. In love? Nah. Not yet."

"Oh, yeah, still new. You don't know what hit you yet." James patted him on the back. "How about we drop the conversation until you come to terms with your love TKO? I actually only came in here to say that I'd be glad to have you on board, son. I'm so glad God saw fit to leave my son on this earth and I might have a chance to work with you in the company I built for my boys."

James hugged him and walked out of his office.

He sat down at the desk.

His desk? One day? Now that was something he never imagined, a nine-to-five day and a desk.

His father's happiness about having him there some-what soothed the feelings of uncertainty he was having. He thought about Samantha again and the way she blew up at him and told him that he needed to be grate-ful he survived the accident and wasn't paralyzed.

For the first time in months he felt a sense of real thankfulness. He could have died. He could have never had the chance to work so closely with his dad—a man he more than admired and wanted to emulate, minus the whole cop thing—and he would have never had the chance to meet Samantha Dash.

It was time to start counting his blessings and take advantage of them, and it was time to stop wasting time.

"How are you feeling today?" Samantha performed the deep-tissue massage on Joel's back and talked to him while she worked. She tried to keep focused on the job at hand and not what kind of cologne Joel was wearing.

She was determined to get whatever was brewing between herself and Mr. Surly back on a patient/practitioner track. She could do it. She would do it.

Except, Mr. Surly wasn't Mr. Surly anymore. Where he was once a sulking, irritable, opinionated-but-still-sexy walking attitude problem, he was now a smiling, devilish, playful, sexy-but-still-opinionated walking, talking temptation.

"I'm doing much better. It's like you and my doctors said, there will be bad days, but I can manage this and make them occur less frequently. You were right.

I should have done the exercises you taught me as soon as I felt the pain coming. I might not have lost an entire day."

Did he just say she was right about something? Oh, goodness, it was worse than she thought. The man could be downright charming when he wanted to be.

He smiled his dimpled grin with a hint of playfulness in his eyes. She nearly swooned. She fought back the urge to let her knees buckle.

"Well, I'm glad you realize that I was right." She smirked, expecting him to come back with one of his smart comments—needing him to come back with one of his zingers so he could help her get it together.

But no... He just smiled again.

"So, I'm thinking I still owe it to you to try your little Chicago-style hot dogs so the battle can finally be put to rest and I can win. So can we reschedule our trip to Willy's?"

Her heart jumped double Dutch in her chest, and her hands all of the sudden felt clammy.

"Oh, sorry, Hightower, when you canceled, we had to consider that a forfeit. You lost this round. Sorry." Not her best work, but it was a pretty good comeback. She tossed him a smirk and patted herself on the back for the save.

If she stayed focus, she could get things back on track.

He just smiled.

She swallowed.

"Since we didn't come up with any rules for the contest, and I had to cancel due to illness, I don't think you can win by forfeit, but if you're refusing to go through with it, then you can forfeit, by all means, and I win."

"*Whatever.* No way." Damn, her competitive streak. "We can do this tonight."

He really let loose his pearly whites then. "Perfect. How about we each pick up hot dogs from our spots and bring them over to my place for the battle?"

His place?

Oh, no, slick talker.

She had seen what could happen at his place when his back was aching and his mother and aunt were downstairs. No way would she trust herself at his place alone.

"We can have the battle on my turf. You can pick up your little Texas wieners from Johnny's and I'll bring the best hot dogs ever to bless New Jersey from Willy's. We can taste them at my place and then you, *my brotha,* are going down!"

His smile widened and his eyes gleamed. "Sounds like a plan."

She frowned.

Why did she think he was thinking about something other than hot dogs?

"You look mighty happy for someone who's about to lose," she quipped.

"Oh, baby girl, that's because I have no intention of losing." He brushed his hand across her cheek and caused a shiver to caress her spine.

She did swoon then, moving with his arm as he pulled it away from her face and stopping herself before completely toppling over.

He grinned and winked. "I play to win."

She barely stifled the gasp that threatened to escape and leave her with no cool points. He played to win, all right, and she knew he had all the capabilities to win a whole lot more than a little hot-dog competition, a lot more indeed....

Chapter 9

After tasting hot dogs from both places, they were at a standstill. The Chicago-style hot dog would always be her favorite, just because they reminded her of home and she always stopped by Willy's when she was feeling homesick. You really couldn't go wrong with a pure-beef, Vienna hot dog, green relish, a pickle spear, tomatoes, peppers and mustard on a poppy-seed hot-dog bun with a sprinkling of celery salt, but she had to admit that those deep-fried cholesterol builders on a bun that Joel loved were also delicious.

"So, I'm thinking we call this one a tie." Joel leaned back on her sofa and smiled at her.

They had moved from her small dining-room table to the couch and were still in mock deliberation.

"I guess that would be okay. Your little hot dogs were kinda good. I could see myself going to Johnny's if Willy's was closed."

He laughed. "Come here, Samantha."

She let out a hiss of breath.

Oh, Lord.

"What do you mean, come here? I'm already here. We're both sitting on the same sofa."

"Come closer to me. Why are you sitting so far away? You scared?"

"Scared of what?"

"Scared of me, of us, of the fact that no matter what you do, we're going to explore this attraction? Take your pick."

Oh, how about all of the above?

"I'm not scared. I just think—"

"Don't do that." He cut her off with his demand.

"Don't do what?"

"Think. Let yourself feel for a minute. Come over here and let yourself feel."

She stared at him. His big bold, brown eyes were daring and sexy in such a potent way. If she didn't think… If she allowed herself to feel… Yeah, she really would be in trouble then.

"I've worked really hard to establish myself in my

career, and while there aren't any rules against me dating a former patient, I have tried to maintain a level of professionalism. But I am attracted to you."

Did I just admit that out loud?

"You're more than attracted to me, Samantha. A woman who is just attracted to a man doesn't come over just to check up on him when he's having a bad-back day. You care about me, sweetheart."

Why does that feel like an understatement?

"Please come here."

She blinked several times and laced her fingers together. She tried to think about what her life would be like when she didn't have to worry about Joel Hightower and all his temptation. Things would be so easy and peaceful then, and boring, and lonely and unsatisfying.

She slid over on the couch, and he placed his arm around her shoulders. She couldn't help but gaze up into his eyes, even though she knew they had some kind of mesmerizing power. How else could she explain the fact she was willing to throw her feelings about professionalism and her fear of getting involved with a man who had a dangerous job to the wind?

She wanted to have this man. Not only did she want him, she was also developing feelings for him. She didn't want to even think about how intense her feelings for Joel were.

He leaned forward, and his lips brushed hers slightly. It was all she needed. Her tongue charged forward, stroking his mouth studiously from the outside to the inside. It was hard not to moan as she trailed the outline of his scandalous smile; difficult not to groan when she savored his tongue and traced the roof of his mouth. So she moaned and groaned with abandon when he pulled her closer and held her tight. His embrace felt sure and steady. It felt right.

Reluctantly, she pulled away. Foolishly, she stared at him, knowing the draw his eyes had on her. He gazed at her with so much emotion and desire she wanted to look away.

He studied her in deep contemplation, nodded and smiled.

"Okay, you look like you're having some kind of personal conversation. What is it? Why are you looking at me like that?"

He shook his head and grinned that little devilish grin of his. "I was just talking with my father earlier today and something finally hit me."

"What?"

He stared at her for a minute and the glimmer she couldn't quite place flashed in his eyes. He opened his mouth and then closed it.

"I'll tell you when you're ready. You're not ready to hear this yet."

"Ooh, now I'm all curious. You have to tell me." She laughed and kissed him softly and slowly. She moved from his mouth to his neck taking pecks and nips. "Tell me."

"Oh, so you want to fight dirty, huh?"

"I'm not a fighter. I'm a lover. Tell me."

He laughed. "A lover, huh?"

"Mmm, hmm, and I'm willing to use the bulk of my loving skills to get you to tell me what has you looking at me all weird."

"That sounds like another battle. I wonder who'll win this one." He murmured the words before covering her mouth in a searing kiss.

Her heart almost jumped out of her chest. The only thing that stopped her from crying uncle or throwing up the white flag was the fact that if she did, it would end the kiss.

"You give up?" He whispered the question right on to her lips.

She got up and straddled his lap. Leaning forward she began to unbutton his shirt and let her hands linger on his muscled chest. She didn't think she'd ever seen anything so virile and masculine. The dark hairs felt soft to the touch and underneath, as hard as steel.

He let out a hiss of breath. She tilted her head and brushed a soft, teasing kiss across his lips before trailing down his chest. She inhaled. His scent had to be a narcotic because she was sure she could easily become addicted.

Who was she kidding? She was already strung out.

The overwhelming urge to taste every inch of his firm, muscled body came over her so suddenly. Before she could even think about it, she was on her knees in front of him on the sofa. She unbuckled his pants and released his sex from captivity.

He was already semi-erect and the size of him made her mouth water. She'd be lying if she said she hadn't thought about what she was about to do, many times.

Taking him in her mouth for the first time let loose a series of emotions in her. On one level, she just wanted to pleasure and please this man more than any other man she had ever known or been with. On another level, she knew she was taking the step to the point of no return. Any arguments she had about keeping a distance were null and void.

She suckled him. Licked him in slow, sure strokes. She savored him and knew without a doubt she could go on tasting him forever.

Lost in her own little world and content to explore him with her mouth while listening to the soft sounds of his sexy moans, she barely felt when he nudged her.

"Sweetheart. Ohh…you're killing me. We have to stop now. Your mouth feels so good, but I won't be able to hang on if you keep this up."

She stopped and stood. Stepping out of her slacks she let them fall to the floor, all the while keeping her eyes on him. Their gazes locked as she performed a striptease for him. The only thing missing was the music. He stood and took off his slacks and shirt, letting his things fall in the small clothes pile that held her belongings.

She noticed he had taken a condom from his wallet.

And there they were, at the point of no return. He guided her to the long chaise end of her sectional sofa and positioned her on the edge with her legs hanging off and her feet firmly planted on the floor. He placed the condom on his erection before getting on his knees between her spread legs. He rested his elbows and the weight of his torso on either side of her on the sofa.

Clearly he'd been doing some research on the best sexual positions for men with back problems.

The anticipation made her stomach flip-flop and her heart race. He just looked at her for what seemed like forever.

"You're beautiful, Samantha. I remember thinking that the first time I saw you."

"No need for sweet talk, Hightower. I think you've pretty much got things in the bag." She arched her hips a little, waiting for him to fill her.

He laughed. "Little Miss Spitfire, you ain't nothing

nice, girl. Here a brother is trying to open up his heart to you and you're trying to rush me."

"How about you save it for the pillow talk, the after-sex cuddling, something like that?"

He chuckled then. "Okay, but I do want to share something with you. You know how you wanted to know what I was thinking? What hit me? Well, I was talking with my dad today and he said that I had the look of a Hightower man in love. He said it would hit me soon and I'd realize it. As I looked at your pretty face this evening, sitting there all cute and contemplative, it hit me. I'm in love."

And with those three words he entered her fully to the hilt, taking her breath away. She had no idea what had robbed her of air, his words or the way he filled her, but she had to remind herself how to breathe just to have the energy to deal with his sure strokes.

Arching up from the sofa, she met him each time his hips came forward.

"You feel so good, sweetheart. God, you feel good."

She widened her legs and wiggled slightly in an effort to get used to his size and girth. She couldn't remember ever feeling so full, so complete.

She allowed her hands to roam the ripples of muscles on his chest, moving from his shoulders to his six-pack abs. Her fingers soaked up his strength and sent shock waves from her arms to her core. He moved his hips with such skill and finesse she soon found it hard to keep clear and coherent thoughts in her head. In fact, her mind seemed to take the background as her body took over.

He cupped her buttocks, pulling her into his powerful thrust. Her back arched off the sofa as the beginnings of the sweetest release she had ever known slowly crept up and down her body, building and building until she had to call out his name. She closed her eyes and shook her head in order to stop herself from letting it all hang out. Her body quaked and quivered, her legs started to shake and her lips parted in silent splendor.

His lips covered hers then and his tongue barreled into her mouth, mimicking the mind-blowing gestures of his hips.

And the fullness consumed her until there was no room. She brought her hands to his face and caressed his handsome profile as she kissed him with everything that was inside of her.

When he moved his mouth from hers, she groaned. When his lips found her nipples and began to suckle one after the other in tandem with the powerful piston of his hips, she moaned. She moaned loud and long as her sex began to tighten and release around him as if she wanted to siphon everything she possibly could from him. His tongue traced and trailed her nipple so seductively, she couldn't hold back any longer and she knew she couldn't take much more.

Could a person be pleasured to death? She had a feeling she might find out if Joel didn't finish soon.

"Joel…" she whispered his name through clenched teeth as her legs—almost as if they had a mind of their own—gripped him in a tight embrace. Hot slick wetness spiraled down, causing her gut to drop and her sex to clench and convulse.

"It feels so good when you come, girl. I could feel that all night…you grabbing me so tight, so tight… Damn, girl." He didn't miss a beat. Continuing his thrusts, he lifted his head and stared at her.

If she could have stopped shaking, she might have been able to get a clearer vision of his handsome face and bright brown eyes. As it was, the only thing she could make out was the wall of mahogany covered steel that made up his chest and arms. She reached up sliding her hands up and down the bulging pipes that made up his arms. The beads of perspiration that layered his masculine body didn't faze her. She relished the slick evidence of how much effort he put into pleasing her. She wasn't afraid of the sweat.

Never… Never had she experienced anything as amazing as making love to Joel Hightower. Each of his strokes seemed to spark fire to her soul. She couldn't even express what his loving had wrenched open in her. She felt like she should say something, but all she could do was get lost in his eyes as she met him thrust for thrust.

Her hips bounced off of the sofa with more urgency than only a moment before. She was reaching, greedily so.

How many orgasms did she think she could get out of one amazing encounter with Joel, anyway? As many as she possibly could, that's how many!

And she was so close, so close.

"Joel. Joel!" His name ripped from her lips in a fevered, impassioned plea.

"It's yours, girl. Take it. Take it!" He moved his hips faster and more deftly, each stroke clearly intended to take her there and back.

And she went on the ride, meeting him and taking him on a ride of her own as she swiveled and pivoted so that he could reach the very depths of her. He moved his hand to the spot that brought her the ultimate pleasure and pressed down as he moved in and out, harder and faster, causing her to clasp him tightly in her thighs as she screamed out her release. He joined her barely seconds later and covered her mouth with a kiss that managed to take the little breath she had left away.

Lying in Samantha's bed and holding her in his arms felt right. It felt more than right. It was perfect.

Things might had been moving faster than he'd been accustomed to in the past, but he realized things couldn't move fast enough, not since it finally hit him.

He smiled and spooned her luscious body closer. The past two-and-a-half months of back-and-forth banter with the mouthy and very sexy physical therapist had caused a sneak attack on his heart. He knew she probably didn't believe him, and he wasn't sure why he felt the need to share the newfound knowledge of his feelings with her.

But he wanted her to know. Hell, he wanted the entire world to know.

He certainly hadn't expected they would make love this evening, but he wasn't about to say no once she stood and did her seductive striptease.

Her spicy and vibrant energy sparked more life in him than he'd felt in months.

He loved it. He loved *her.*

"You know, I won't hold you to any of that stuff you said, Joel. I know things get said in the heat of the moment and—"

He kissed the back of her neck and pulled her closer. Her words halted and she shivered.

"That's what I meant by 'you weren't ready to hear it,' but don't worry. I'm dedicated to making you believe it."

He could feel her pause, could almost see the

wheels turning in her head. Her back was to him so he couldn't see her face, but he didn't have to see it to know she was probably talking herself into a million reasons why he couldn't possibly have meant what he said, a million excuses about professionalism and how they shouldn't be together.

Well, she could drop all that nonsense now. He wasn't giving her up for anything or anyone. He also thought about the comments she made about her father and the way he died. The last thing he wanted to do was bring her father into bed with them at that moment, but he did feel the need to be closer to her.

"Tell me something about yourself, Samantha. I already know you're the best physical therapist in the state of Jersey—"

"I'm the best physical therapist in the world," she teasingly interrupted as she wiggled her hips.

He groaned, but he didn't move away. He relished the seductive tingles that pulsed through his body. He felt alive holding her.

"Okay, the best in the world… Tell me something I don't know. I know you were a daddy's girl and your pops was a cop. What about your mom? What does she do?"

Her wiggling stopped, and he could feel her back straighten. "My mom's in Chicago. She…ah…never really recovered after losing my father… She took it hard."

Instinctively, he pulled her closer to him. She felt so amazing in his arms that he never wanted to let her go. Each curve of her body felt like bountiful perfection.

"She drinks… A lot…" Her short, stilted words hinted that she would rather not be talking about her mother, but she continued.

"From the time my father was murdered, she hit the bottle hard and hasn't stopped. I've tried a lot of things over the years to try and get her to stop, but she won't." Her voice quivered a little, and he heard her take a big gasp of air.

"I tried to make her go to rehab, but she wouldn't do it. I've stopped talking to her. I've threatened not to visit her. I've hounded her. I've done so much through the years. I think that's why I was so happy to get in to graduate school in New Jersey. It meant I could finally leave home."

"I'm sorry, sweetheart." He didn't know what else to say, so he just held her tight.

"It's okay. It is what it is. She just couldn't cope with my father's death. His dangerous job cost him his life, and it cost me a father and a mother. I lost them both to that robber's bullet."

Again he had no idea what to say. She clearly had an issue with her father's job. Would she have an issue with him returning to firefighting? Would it squash their barely starting relationship?

It couldn't. He refused to let it. Knowing what he was up against, he vowed to make her see that they belonged together.

He pressed his lips to the back of her neck and planted soft kisses. With his hands wrapped around her, he cupped her breast and began a slow circular tease on her nipple moving from one to the other until they each pointed out in hardened peaks. He allowed his other hand to move down the front of her body. He spread his fingers over her stomach, caressing it lovingly. Moving lower, he found the slick folds of her sex and dived in, letting his hand soak up the intense heat.

He had no idea how long he familiarized himself with her body and its responses. The entire concept of time seemed foreign, and he was ruled only by the *"aahs"* and *"oohs"* of pleasure escaping her lips as she pushed back into him and wiggled her bottom.

Spooning never felt this good. Her voluptuous behind moved against his sex, and soon he was standing at full attention. He continued his play with her breasts and sex, even though his erection demanded attention because he loved the way she moaned as her body shook and another orgasm caused her liquid warmth to cover his fingers. He could ignore his needs knowing he was bringing her so much pleasure.

He allowed his fingers to explore her more fully, dipping and delving into her depths, driving himself to the edge of insanity right along with her. He added another finger, circling and stretching her as his thumb lightly pushed and pressed her pleasure spot. His other hand tweaked her nipple. He loved the way it hardened to a point in his hand.

Soft shudders caused her shoulders to move against him in need and surrender. But he wasn't ready to let her off. He continued to work her with his hand, loving the sticky, sweet evidence of her desire.

"Joel…please…" She panted the words just as her back arched, her head tilted and more of her fire soaked his hand. "Please!" Her plea vibrated through the room, much like her thighs vibrated around his arms, holding him as the last bits of her orgasm coursed through her.

He continued his purposeful feeling, his determined exploration. He might not be able to totally make love to her the way he would have when he had a healthy back, but he could damn sure bring her pleasure unlike anything she had ever experienced. In fact, that was his new goal. Each time he felt her release, it sparked the hyper adrenaline in him that he hadn't felt in the many months since he'd fought his last fire. He felt alive. And he was going to make her feel it, too.

He nibbled the back of her neck as he continued to stroke her. Her breathing slowed to soft, shuddering pants until her back straightened and her sex clenched his fingers. She moaned and cried out as she threw her head back into his chest.

This time, the feel of her tight, slick hold was his undoing. He had to feel her tightening around him like that again, but he wanted to be deep inside of her when it happened. He removed his hand and rolled over.

"Top drawer," she directed with the same lilt.

He opened the top drawer of her nightstand and found the protection. Quickly shielding himself, he pulled her back into his arms, spooning her again. Her soft round behind cushioned him and made him think of the warm sweetness he'd left only moments ago.

He tilted her hips slightly and entered the heat of her womanhood. He felt her tighten around him almost immediately. They moved slowly and surely, in sync and as one. He was able to move deeper and deeper until he didn't know where he stopped and she began. If ever there was a perfect fit, this was certainly it.

Each thrust felt like a homecoming, each withdrawal a loss. He pulled out to the tip. Breathed. Thrust back into the hilt. Hissed. He lost count how many times he repeated these actions. He only knew that he couldn't get enough of the soft warm feel of her engulfing his manhood and soaking him with her desire.

If he didn't know his own history, he would have sworn that he had never made love before. But the truth was he had never made love like *this* before.

He slowed his stroke, savoring the tight, slick heat of her. However, the hard pounding double beats in his chest and the unrelenting pulse throbbing all over his body told him it wouldn't be long before he gave in to the call of bliss.

He cupped her breasts and kneaded them using them to pull her tighter to his body. She increased her pace, bouncing back with a fervor and desire that seemed to possess her. She pressed back, riding him with each soulful swivel of her hips. Each move made him squeeze and hold her tighter, made him thrust harder and faster.

Soon she screamed out his name and it was only a matter of seconds before he screamed out her name, as well. The satisfied sigh they each released echoed throughout the room.

"That feels nice. You're so much gentler when you're away from the clinic. You need to work it like that all the time." Joel teased Samantha as she finished massaging his back.

They were lounging in his bedroom after watching

a movie and having Chinese food. After only a week, he knew two things. He loved sharing his space with Samantha, and he was going to work on making sure he was able to keep her there.

She sucked her teeth and pinched his arm, hard.

"Ouch. You're supposed to help, not hurt."

"That's what happens when you mouth off at your physical therapist, Hightower. She might just rub you the wrong way."

"*Ha, ha, ha.* You've got jokes. Bring that sassy mouth of yours over here."

She leaned forward and gave him a brief peck on the lips.

"I should probably head home. We have your family's cookout tomorrow. I'm still not sure I should go.…"

"What do you mean? Of course you should go. It's just a little family get-together. We have them whenever we can during the summer, especially when we can get a bunch of us off from work at the same time. It'll be fun. Plus, my mom specifically said, 'Bring her to the cookout,' and then there's the more important reason, *I* want you there." Joel turned and sat up. He pulled her into his arms and onto his lap before covering her mouth with a kiss.

He would never get enough of her. Her luscious lips opened to him immediately, and he smiled. Her tongue twirled like a tornado, leaving him devastated in the best way. He couldn't envision rebuilding if he ever lost her. No kisses had ever floored him that way, and he knew none ever would.

She pulled away, panting, and it was good to see that she had been as affected as he was.

"I think we're moving too fast." She tried to move from his lap.

He held her tight. "And I don't think we're moving fast enough." He slid the sleeveless T-shirt she was wearing off her shoulders and brushed his lips across her collarbone. "For example, you really should be naked by now."

She grinned. "That's not what I'm talking about, smarty-pants."

"I know, but you should still be naked. I think much better when you are."

"Nasty boy…"

He took her nipple in his mouth and suckled. If he had to work her until all thoughts of "too fast" were permanently erased from her pretty little head, then so be it. He was a man on a mission.

"Mmm… How am I supposed to have a conversation with you when you're doing that? Mmm…" Her held fell back, and her back arched, feeding him more and more of the delectable chocolate morsels of her nipples.

He moved from one nipple to the other, feasting until she writhed on his lap and cried out in pleasure.

"Still wanna go slow?" he whispered in her ear as she came down from her peak.

She shook her head. "No way." She smiled. "Hey…why aren't we naked?"

Chapter 10

"No, Mama, I can't come home until late fall. I told you I had to wait until I get more vacation time."

"Well, I think it's horrible I only get to see my child once or twice a year. You really need to get a job closer to home, Sammie. Tomorrow isn't promised. You'd think a person with only one parent left would get that."

The snippiness of her mother's voice made Samantha's skin prickle.

It was the sober and sarcastic mother on the phone. Not that she could have a real conversation that wasn't full of hurt feelings and accusations with Veronica

Dash in any of her incarnations, but at least she could understand the words coming out of her mother's mouth when she wasn't inebriated.

Samantha had given up trying to make her mother get her act together. It was just too taxing on her mind and spirit. Getting accepted into graduate school in New Jersey and getting a job there felt like a lifesaver because she could no longer watch her mother drink her life away. It was bad enough seeing it twice a year and listening to it on the phone.

"Mama, you know I love you, and I spend every vacation I get in Chicago." She sighed in frustration. "I could be taking a trip to the Bahamas or Jamaica, you know."

"Oh…I'm so lucky my only child spends a couple of weeks a year with me. Whoopie! First my husband was murdered and I have to grow old without my soul mate and then my child decides to move to another state and I have to die… Oh, just forget it then, Samantha Elaine Dash! Just stay the hell in New Jersey forever for all I care."

Click.

Being hung up on by one's mother on a regular basis had to have some kind of cumulative hardening effect. There had been a time when she would have been so distressed by it she would have called right back, apologizing and begging for forgiveness.

Not today.

Today, she simply swallowed and placed the cordless back on the charger. The only thing Samantha learned she could do was hope and pray her mother made a change before her drinking caused irrevocable health problems. Or something worse.

Her mind traced back to her mother's use of the word *die*. She never mentioned death or dying before in her rants, just her loneliness and misery.

Just as Samantha was about to pick up the phone and see if there was more to her mother's latest phone call, the phone rang again.

It must be her. This time I'll try to be more open and see if there is anything really wrong. She calls a lot anyway, but maybe this recent onslaught of phone calls has a deeper meaning behind them.

"Hello, sweetheart."

Definitely not Mom…

Samantha couldn't help the big old grin working its way across her face.

After making love with Joel on Wednesday, they had fallen into a slow and easy pattern. Things hadn't become all weird in their relationship, and she was convinced they would be able to finish out the last week of his therapy without drama. She still wasn't sure how she felt about taking a chance and starting a relationship with a man who could be heading back to a dangerous job. And she wasn't sure what was in store, but she was more or less ready to take the ride.

They had made love several times during the rest of the week at either her apartment or his town house, and he'd even gotten her to agree to attend a cookout at his parents' home for Saturday. To calm her nerves, she reminded herself that it was just a little family get-together, nothing major. So what if she was about to meet everyone in his immediate family today.

Today, she thought as she realized her mother's phone call had totally taken her mind away from the task of finding something decent to wear.

"Hey, you…" She couldn't keep the desire from her voice. It just seemed to go hand in hand with talking to Joel.

"So, are you just about ready? I was about to leave and come pick you up when I figured I should call, given how late you crept out of here last night."

She smiled in remembrance. "I didn't creep out of there. I just knew if I stayed, I wouldn't get any rest, and I wanted to get my beauty sleep before meeting all your folks."

He chuckled. "You don't need beauty sleep. You're gorgeous, but are you dressed and ready to go?"

She laughed. "I think I'll only need about an extra half hour. I'm trying to pick out the right outfit."

"Why don't you wear those denim shorts you were wearing when I saw you at the grocery store… Oh, never mind, if I come to your place and you're wearing those shorts we might not make it to the cookout."

"Look at you. You're full of the devil, as my grandmother used to say."

"And you in the shorts ain't nothing nice, girl… You liable to hurt a brotha, so wear whatever you want. But know this, if you are wearing those shorts, I can't be responsible for the beast you'll unleash."

"Mmm… Now that sounds tempting. I like your beast. He's rather cute."

"And insatiable. My mother would have a fit if I didn't bring you to the cookout after she more or less demanded you come when she met you the night you stopped by my place. And she's been calling me every day since to remind me to bring you."

"Your mother is so sweet. Tell me…will your dear aunt be there, too?"

"Yes, but you don't need to worry about her, between her beef with my mom and my new sister-in-law she'll barely have time to bother you at all."

"Oh, great!" she said as sarcastically as she could.

He laughed. "Plus, I'm sure Little Miss Spitfire can handle my aunt just fine. Just put her in check like you're always trying to check me."

"*Trying* to check? Boy, please… You see how I

whipped you into shape. You've had a complete attitude overhaul thanks to me."

He really cracked up then. "See, nothing nice... I'll pick you up in about forty-five minutes, hot stuff."

"Okay. Bye."

She hung up and finished raiding her closet for something fly to wear.

She had decided to wear a pair of peach linen shorts with a matching short-sleeved jacket and a sleeveless white silk camisole underneath. The summer suit was dressy casual, and she could take off the little jacket if it got too hot out. Joel's eyes had popped out of his head when she'd opened her door, and it made her feel as beautiful as he kept telling her she was.

The ride over to his parents' home was relaxed once they agreed on which CD to listen to. They both listened to hip-hop, but he preferred Jay-Z while she vibed to Nas. He was a die-hard Mary J. Blige fan and refused to buy her argument that Keyshia Cole represented the new generation's version of the queen of hip-hop soul. The more she thought about it, the more she realized they actually had more in common than not, including the fact they were each *very* opinionated.

Luckily, they both liked Algebra Blessett and her

music was in a class by itself, so they mellowed out on the short drive from her apartment in to his parents' huge home on the East Side of Paterson, listening to Algebra.

She tried not to be nervous as she entered the backyard of the Hightowerses Tudor-style minimansion right across the street from East Side Park. She had driven by these beautiful homes in Paterson before, but she had never been in one. The home had a stately elegance that was breathtaking. Everything from the leaded glass to the beautiful wood built-ins gave the home an old-money feel. They had also done some remodeling, which was evident in the state-of-the-art kitchen. The teakwood deck in the backyard was nothing to sneeze at, either.

"Your home is gorgeous, Mrs. Hightower," Samantha gushed after coming back from a quick tour with Joel.

"Thank you, sweetie. It's been the family home for several generations. My husband, James, grew up here and his father before him. I'm glad you were able to make it. Let me introduce you to everyone." Celia cut her eyes in Sophie's direction. "You already met my sister-in-law, Sophie. This is my husband, James Hightower." She pointed to a man who could only be described as an older version of the four other handsome Hightower men sitting around the large teak table on the deck.

They were all tall, deep-chocolate versions of heaven, and the finest of them all had his arm around her.

Joel continued to hold her close as his mother introduced her to Patrick, Lawrence, Jason and his wife, Penny.

Penny had to be the prettiest woman she had ever seen. She had the oddest color eyes and these long, golden-brown sisterlocks that made Samantha question why she continued to do two-strand twists in her own hair when she could be wearing some fierce sisterlocks like Penny's.

Penny's mother, Carla, and father, Gerald, were also there, as well as two friends from California, Maritza and Terrell.

She nodded politely and said hello to everyone, but with each new person she started to get this feeling of dread. What was she doing attending a cookout at her patient's home and meeting his family as if they had some kind of future together? Hadn't she sworn off ever dating a man with a dangerous job?

Even if they did have a future, wasn't it too soon to play "meet the folks"? Shouldn't they date for a while first?

What have you got yourself into?

She took a deep breath and tried to keep the smile

plastered on her face while her heart started playing a conga in her chest.

It was at that moment she felt a slight reassuring squeeze on her shoulder. She tilted her head and gazed right into Joel's expressive brown eyes and what she saw there, oddly enough, calmed her.

She knew if she had seen that level of loving, caring and devotion in his eyes weeks before this moment she would have ran in the other direction, but seeing it now just made her smile and nod.

"So, you're the girl who has my son walking around here with the look." James Hightower stood behind his wife and wrapped her in his arms.

"The look?" She glanced at Joel again.

"Yes." James nodded in Jason's direction. "Take a look at my son Jason over there."

She glanced over at Jason. He was grinning up a storm and couldn't seem to take his eyes off his beautiful wife. She turned back to James with a quizzical expression. She had no idea what she was supposed to be seeing.

"Oops. She doesn't recognize it yet. Guess you've got your work cut out for you." James winked at Joel.

Joel smiled and shrugged. "Don't worry. I'm more than capable of helping her see it. I'm the only man for the job."

James nodded. "I have no doubt. Nothing can stop a Hightower when he has that kind of focus. Ask your mama." He gave Celia a slow peck on the lips, lingering just enough to cause everyone to stare and then went back over to the grill.

James Hightower seemed more interested in checking out his wife than those bratwursts on the grill.

He'd better start paying attention to the grill. The only thing I like burnt at a cookout is my hot dog, and even those I don't like too burnt....

It was cute though to see an older man still so much in love and devoted to his wife he couldn't take his eyes off her.

She turned to Joel, who was gazing at her.

"Your family is nice," she said in an attempt to break his stare.

"Yes, they're cool. I think I'll keep them."

"It must have been so cool growing up in a big family with older and younger siblings."

"It was. I liked knowing they would always have my back, even though sometimes I just wanted them to mind their own business. I'm sure they've felt that way about me at times, too. You were an only child, right?"

"Yep, just me and Mom after Daddy died, and both of them were only children, so I didn't even have cousins...."

She just pursed her lips and cut off her own words. Sitting there basking in the closeness of his family, she didn't want to call attention to her own dysfunctional relationship with her mom or her lack of family.

The Hightowers had it right. They were what a family was supposed to be, and at that moment, she just wanted to fit in.

"Samantha, would you like to come on in the kitchen with us to finish up the side dishes? We can have girl talk while the guys finish the grilling." Celia Hightower came over and it was hard not to be won over by her smiling face and pleasant demeanor.

"Sure, I'd love to." She got up and followed Celia, Penny and Maritza into the kitchen.

Celia stopped before opening the screen door. She opened her mouth and closed it again before taking great pain to speak. "Sophie, would you like to join us?"

"No, I wouldn't." Sophie turned her head sharply after giving off a haughty expression of disdain that seemed to stop and rest on each of them. "Too many...cooks... Mmmph."

Celia smiled an easy and relieved smile. "What about you, Carla?"

Penny's mother was cuddled next to Penny's dad, and it didn't look like she was moving anytime soon.

"Y'all know I don't cook, but y'all need to hurry up and get this party started. I'm hungry."

"Eat some chips or something." Penny rolled her eyes and shook her head.

"I don't want no chips. I want food. *F-O-O-D. Food.*" Carla rolled her eyes at Penny and then snuggled back up with Gerald.

"Okay, Carla, we'll have things ready in a sec." Celia shook her head and kept walking into the house.

"My mother is a nut," Penny said, rolling her eyes.

"Your mother is hilarious. Ain't no shame in her game, that's for sure." Maritza laughed. "She cracks me up. I love Carla. She's off the chain!"

"Carla is real, and she tells it like she sees it, that's for sure," Celia said. "Okay, Penny, you're on pasta salad, and Maritza can help you with that. I guess we can share the family recipe with her since she'll end up with Terrell one day and he's like a son to me, so that makes her family."

"Terrell? No way. He works my last nerves. *El stupido.* Argh!" Maritza turned to Penny. "Why didn't you tell me he was going to be here, *chica?* I didn't know he was coming until he had the *nerve* to call me and to try and tell me what to wear to the cookout! Like I don't know how to dress myself?"

Celia and Penny exchanged knowing glances.

"Anyway, you're just like family, so we'll trust you

with the family recipes," Celia offered. "And you, Samantha sweetie, can help me with my signature potato salad."

Samantha laughed at the still-frowning face of Maritza. "Are you sure you want to share the family recipes with me, Mrs. Hightower?"

"Of course, Samantha, both you and Maritza are family, whether you realize it or not." Celia chuckled softly to herself, and a devilish little gleam lit her eyes.

Like mother like son, Samantha thought as she washed her hands in the sink.

She thought Maritza and Penny looked familiar and had written it off as simply their stunning photographic looks. As it turned out, the best friends were former video girls and they had actually met on a rap-video set. She must have seen them in a video or something.

Samantha finished mixing up the potato salad and hoped it came out okay because she did not want to be the person who jacked up the potato salad at the cookout.

Maritza took a seat on the barstool next to her. "Anyway, can you believe this woman had to come and snatch up the second-hottest Hightower brother?"

"That's right, second hottest!" Penny slapped her best friend five. "Y'all better recognize. My baby, Jason, is the hottest by far."

"All my sons are hot, including Terrell, who is just

like a son to me since he, Penny and Jason spent so much time here driving me nuts when they were kids." Celia nudged Penny with her elbow.

Maritza scowled at the mention of Terrell's name.

"What woman snatched up the second-hottest Hightower? Is she here? Who's the second hottest in your opinion, Maritza? I think I have to side with Mrs. Hightower on this one. They're all equally hot." As far as Samantha was concerned, Joel was really the finest of them all, but she wasn't hardly about to say that.

"You, chica." Maritza laughed. "You came up in here today with the second-hottest Hightower, Joel," Maritza said, and drew out Joel's name in a sing-song voice.

The proper thing to do, since he was her patient and not technically her man, would have been to tell Maritza that Joel was still a free agent. After all, they weren't *together,* together. And sure, they had this chemistry and the sex was sizzling, crackling, spark-ling hot... Then there was the fact he had already sort of professed his love for her, but that was right before sex. She couldn't count that.

In all honesty, she shouldn't have the desire to tell Little Miss Video Model Maritza to stay away from her man. He wasn't her man...right?

She could neither confirm nor deny, and she wasn't about to give Maritza a free pass to go after the hottest

Hightower at the cookout, so she just smiled and shrugged.

"Look at her. I'm scared of you, girl! You gave me the look like, *sorry, chick, he is mine.* Did y'all see how she looked at me?"

Celia just beamed, and Penny smiled.

"All right, ladies, let's take this food out there before Carla starts giving us a piece of her mind," Celia said with a light chuckle.

"Goodness knows we don't want to get her started," Penny offered.

They carried the various salads and side dishes outside and put them on the big teak picnic table.

As she sliced into her perfectly grilled chicken, Samantha thought it was a good thing they went inside to finish up the side dishes or Mr. Hightower would have burned up the food gazing at his wife.

"Mama, as usual you put your foot in this potato salad," Joel's older brother Lawrence exclaimed.

"I didn't make the potato salad." Celia winked at Samantha.

"They always get you like that." The oldest Hightower son, Patrick, smirked at Lawrence. "Penny made it."

Penny shook her head. "Nope, I didn't make it, either."

"Okay... Wait..." Lawrence eyed Maritza and

smiled. "Don't tell me, Miss Maritza "I Don't Believe In Cooking" made it."

"No. Samantha made it." Maritza batted her eyes at Lawrence, and Samantha could only assume she had set her sights on the next-hottest Hightower brother.

"Aww, man… Another little brother lucks out and gets a pretty girl who can cook like Mama." Lawrence winked at Patrick and then turned to Samantha. "So, just how close are you with my kid brother Joel? Because in case you hadn't noticed, I'm way better looking, and—"

"Whatever, Casanova Wack. She's taken." Joel placed his arm around her. "Find your own woman."

Samantha smiled. The Hightowers were a riot, and they really made her wish her childhood could have been different. It would have been so cool to have brothers and sisters, a loving mom and a dad who'd been around.

"Penny, how long have you had your sisterlocks? I've been contemplating either getting sisterlocks of just locs." Samantha couldn't get over how beautiful Penny's hair looked. It made her think about doing something more permanent herself. "I've worn my natural hair in two-strand twists since graduate school while I've thought about making the commitment. I think I'm finally ready to do it, especially after seeing your beautiful sisterlocks."

"Oh, you should definitely consider them. I love mine. I've had them for about six years now."

"Mmmph." Sophie rolled her eyes and sucked her teeth in disgust. "A bunch of nappy-headed harlots.... Does anyone believe in perms anymore? I mean, really, what're you going to do when you have children? Let them run around here nappy headed, too? I will *not* have Hightower children running around here with nappy heads."

No. She. Did. Not. Did that old woman just pull a Don Imus on me?

"Now, Sophie, don't start." James gave his sister a stern look.

"Yes, Sophie, really!" Celia shook her head.

"Sophie needs to chill before she get stole on." Carla folded her hands across her chest.

Samantha slanted her right eye and folded her arms across her chest. The fact she and Joel were a long way from even thinking about kids was neither here nor there, and the fact Sophie may or may not have been talking about her in her little rant against the reign of the nappy heads was beside the point.

The only thing that really mattered in the moment was Sophie Hightower must have lost her damn mind, and Samantha was just the person to help her find it.

"First of all, *Sophie,* I find your comments not only insulting but pitifully self-loathing. There is nothing wrong with people choosing to wear their hair in its natural state. Just like there is nothing wrong with people deciding to wear their hair chemically straightened. I find the variety of textures represented at this table alone beautiful, because I find black people beautiful.

"And for the record, I'm happy to be nappy. If I ever have kids, they will wear their natural nappy hair until they are old enough to make decisions about how they want to represent themselves in the world."

Samantha rambled out her words so fast and so furiously she barely took a breath. It was only after she finished and was putting a piece of chicken in her mouth that she realized she had just told off Joel's aunt. His father's sister.

Guess who won't be invited back to the family dinner.

She glanced around the table and just as she thought, all eyes were on her. She put her eyes back on her plate. She couldn't look them in the eyes. She didn't even bother looking at Joel. He was probably embarrassed that he brought her along.

Carla started a slow clap.

Penny was right: her mother was a nut.

Now Carla was calling even more attention to what had just happened, and all Samantha wanted to do was crawl under the table.

"Ha! You tell her, new girl! Ha! You finally got one

who will stand up to your ole hateful behind. She ain't gonna cut you no slack like Penny did. It's *on* now. I like her. Joel, you need to go on and *wife* her like the kids say. She's a keeper. Ha!" Carla stopped clapping and let out a gut-busting laugh.

Samantha decided to take a chance and look at the folks around the table again. Everyone at the table seemed to be trying to hold back their laughter. Everyone but Sophie. She was shooting the serious evil eye in Samantha's direction.

"So, Samantha, are you from around here?" Patrick made an obvious attempt to change the subject.

"Yeah, I don't sense a Jersey accent." Lawrence eyed her inquisitively.

Smooth transition. She would have to thank them later.

Although, an even better move would have been to engage someone else in conversation and take the spotlight off her completely, but she had to work with what they'd given her.

"I'm from Chicago. I came out here for graduate school and I got my MS in Occupational Therapy and Doctor of Physical Therapy degree from Seton Hall University. Since I ended up getting a job in the area, I decided to stay."

"Chi-town, huh? So how are you liking Jersey?" Jason asked.

"I like it. I love my job. I've met some really cool people. It's nice." She nodded and smiled, hoping they would find someone else to talk to soon.

"What made you decide to become a physical therapist?" Terrell asked.

"I've always been interested in the health-care field. I realized early on that nursing wasn't for me, and the idea of actually seeing a lot of blood didn't really move me—" she shuddered briefly before continuing "—but helping people with the after stages of recovery after the nurses and medical doctors have cleaned up all the blood and gore, that worked for me."

"Mmmph," Sophie rolled her eyes.

Here she goes again. This woman won't quit. Ignore her.

"Do you think it's professional to be dating your patients, *Samantha?*" Sophie drew her name out and released it in a hiss.

"Aunt Sophie, let it go." Joel narrowed his eyes on his aunt.

"Yeah, Sophie, let it go. You've just been allowed back at the house after the way you treated Penny." There was an edge in Jason's voice as he addressed his aunt.

"I'm not letting anything go, and neither should you all. I mean, really, I'd like to see these DPT and

MS degrees she claims she has, 'cause it looks like she is abusing her professional relationship to gain an *M-R-S* degree." Sophie shook her head and let out a mocking laugh. "You better be careful, Joel. Mmmph. Physical therapist, my behind. More like a cheap masseuse. Professional? Mmmph… I bet she's a pro, all right."

"That's enough, Aunt Sophie. If you can't respect my guest, you are going to have to leave," Joel snapped.

"Ha! Don't let the doorknob hit ya, Sophie," Carla taunted.

"Sophie, please just shut up," Celia implored.

"I'm not shutting up while you allow your sons to ruin our family name with their poor taste in women, am I the only one who can see what is going on here? You're building up your little nappy-headed army of harlots, Celia, but I won't be silenced by the likes of you."

Celia pursed her lips and then turned to her husband.

James got up and gave his wife a peck on the check. "Babe, wrap my food up for me while I take my sister home." He stood by his sister. "You're going to have to stop this, Sophie. You're getting ridiculous. Worse and worse."

Sophie huffed and gave Celia, Penny and Samantha the evil eye before standing.

"I wonder if your place of employment knows you are whoring yourself with your patients." Sophie spun around and made her grand exit with that statement.

Whoring!

Samantha made a move to get up from the table only to be halted by Joel's hand.

She glared at him. It was his fault after all.

"Well, I think you handled Sophie very well, *chica,*" Maritza said.

"For once I have to agree with Maritza. You held it down with class and black power. 'I find your comments insulting and self-loathing,'" Terrell offered with a chuckle.

"Don't be agreeing with me. Find your own opinion." Maritza rolled her eyes at Terrell.

"Okay, enough arguing for one day. I can't wait until you two get together," Jason teased.

Maritza crossed her arms, and Terrell started fiddling with the food on his plate.

"Carla, pass me the potato salad," Gerald said. The man had been quiet most of the afternoon. He seemed content just being there and taking everything in.

"Just cause you put a ring on my finger don't mean you got a maid, bro. Your hands can reach." Carla twisted her lips to the side. "I'll tell you, these men forget they can do things once they get a woman to do things for them."

Penny let out an exasperated sigh. "Mommy, it's rude to reach. Pass Pops the potato salad."

"Rude, spude. Whatever. We all family now. The Hightowers already know how we do." Carla folded her arms and twisted her lips to the side.

Penny gave Carla an intense, reproachful stare.

"Oh, brother! Fine." Carla passed Gerald the bowl.

"Thank you so much, love of my life," Gerald teased his woman with a smile.

"This party is boring. Y'all ain't got no music?" Carla complained.

Penny shook her head.

Samantha looked away from the various interactions. At least she was out of the spotlight. She looked up at Joel and found him staring at her. Well, maybe she wasn't completely out of the spotlight yet.

"Hold your horses, Carla. I have music. James got me one of those iPod thingies and he put all these oldies but goodies on it. I have it right over here." Celia got up and turned on her iPod. "I'll put it on shuffle so it will just mix up the songs."

"All you got on there is old songs? I wanna hear some new music." Carla folded her arms across her chest. "I wanna crank dat soldier or lean wit' it rock wit' it—"

The music started wafting through the air, and Carla stopped short.

"Oh… Hey, wait a minute. That used to be my cut!" Carla screamed and then started singing. "It only takes a minute, girl… To fall in love…to fall in love…" She grabbed Gerald's hand and they started dancing.

"Hey, I remember my dad used to play this song all the time. Who sings this?" Maritza stood and started swaying to the music.

"Tavares." Terrell watched her move as he answered the question.

Samantha could tell that there was definitely something going on with those two even if they didn't know it yet.

"Will you dance with me?" Joel whispered his request in her ear.

She stood, and he wrapped her in his arms. They were probably moving way too slow, but it didn't matter. What mattered was the way it felt to be in his arms.

"I never knew how true the words to this song were before now." Joel planted a kiss on her forehead. "It only takes a minute."

She couldn't help but smile. Truth be told it hadn't even taken her that long.…

Holding Samantha in his arms and dancing to the old-school music felt right. The rest of the people at the cookout seemed to disappear.

"I apologize for how rudely my aunt Sophie behaved. She has always been a bit of a snob, but she seems to be getting worse in her old age. It's like she's taken this longtime rivalry she has with my mom and extended it to any other woman within range— at least the ones she hasn't handpicked and tried to push off on us."

"Your mother must be a saint. If I had to put up with that mean old woman for the amount of time your mom has, I might be in jail." Samantha shook her head as she spoke, and he could tell she was still rather heated because her words sped out of her mouth.

She paused, took a breath and continued. "And what is the deal with you all continuing to let her come around when clearly she is a menace. One day, she's going to insult the wrong person. Everyone isn't as nice as me."

He chuckled.

"What are you laughing at? I'm nice. I don't care what you say. I'm as sweet as can be, and come to think of it, your aunt really can try the patience of a saint, because she certainly tried me today."

He really let loose a gut-busting laugh then. "Baby, you are sweet, but I told you before, you ain't nothing nice. Girl, I'm scared of you… Not too many people can say they left Sophie Hightower speechless. You had her shook for a minute there, and I'm sure that if you weren't worried about making an impression on the family, you would have really told her off when she went on her second tirade."

"Fat lot of good it did me. My limited constraint didn't stop me from letting her get to me, but she actually called us nappy-headed harlots! Who calls people that?"

"Like I said, girl, I'm scared of you…but I'm also very proud of you. I love you."

She tilted her head and gazed at him as he pulled her close and swayed to the music.

"So, you've met my immediate family. When do I get to meet yours? Does your mom come visit a lot from Chicago?"

"My mom? No. Why would you want to meet my family? Trust me we are *nothing* like you Hightowers. It's probably best to just leave it at that." She yawned.

"Are you getting tired?"

"A little."

"I hope you're not too tired. I'm thinking we can head back to your place after this and spend some time further exploring our relationship…" He let his words trail off but his eyes spoke volumes.

When her tongue darted out and wet her lower lip before she gulped and swallowed, he knew that she had gotten his message loud and clear.

"We can definitely head back to my place. I'm in the mood for some exploration. In fact, I aim to be well traveled." Her saucy smirk moved from her sensual lips to her soulful eyes.

He smiled. He loved how quick she was on her feet and how she rolled with him verbally. "With me as your tour guide, you're in for the trip of your life."

He thought he had her stumped for a comeback until after a half a second when a sly grin formed on her kissable lips.

She eyed him as if she wanted to taste. "If you're driving, I'll take the ride anytime, anyplace, anywhere."

Chapter 11

When they got back to her apartment that evening, she saw her message light blinking but decided not to check them. She didn't want Joel to hear the thousand-and-one drunken messages from her mom, especially after they had spent the day with his wonderful, loving—with the exception of Aunt Sophie—family. If Joel heard her mother's nasty messages, he would see how dysfunctional her family really was.

She plopped down on her sofa instead and Joel sat down right next to her.

"My family really loves you."

"Yeah, I think your aunt Sophie would beg to differ on that one."

She wanted to laugh and shrug what Sophie had said off, but she couldn't. The mean old woman had basically echoed some of the concerns Samantha already had about dating Joel, and then there was her vow never to get involved with a man who had a dangerous job. Maybe Sophie's hateful behavior was really a blessing in disguise?

"You handled yourself well with my aunt, and Mom had you in the kitchen and gave you the secret to her potato salad. You do realize she has pretty much given you a life sentence, don't you?" That sexy smile crossed his face, and his eyes gleamed.

"You pretty much have to end up with one of her sons, and since I have no intention of letting Lawrence or Patrick have you, you're stuck with me."

Luckily the phone rang before she had to respond.

She got up to get the phone, hoping it wasn't her mother. The last thing she wanted was for Joel to hear her having one of those dreadful conversations with her mom.

"Hello."

"Where have you been, girl? I haven't heard from you all weekend." Jenny's peppy voice boomed through the phone line.

Jenny had to be the nosiest woman on the face of the planet.

"It's only Saturday, Jenny, and I told you I had a cookout to go to."

Jenny made a *"pooh-pooh"* sound. "Yeah, I know, and you got me waiting all night by the phone to find out how it went. I bet his family just adored you. So, how was it?"

"I have company. Can I call you back?"

"Company? Is he still there?" She could feel Jenny smiling through the phone. "I guess things went well then—"

"Yeah, I'll call you tomorrow, or we'll chat at work on Monday."

"Monday! You can't make me wait till Monday to get the goods, girl. Come on!"

Samantha could almost see Jenny bouncing up and down and pouting.

"Okay, then, Jenny. I'll talk with you later on. Give the kids a hug and a kiss for me and tell Walt I said hello."

"You ain't right. You're just an evil little wench."

"*Ha, ha.* Girl, you so crazy. Bye." Samantha hung up the phone and hoped Jenny had sense enough not to call back.

Instead of sitting back on the sofa with Joel, she continued to stand. Stretching, she made a production of yawning. The last thing she wanted was for him to go. She would have loved to spend one more night in his arms, but ending things before they got out of hand was the best route.

"Boy, I'm tired. It was a long day, huh?" She yawned again.

He stood up and walked over to where she was standing. "Yes, it was a long day. I'm ready for bed myself." He pulled her into his arms. "What about you?"

"I'm ready for bed, too…" Yawn. "Mmm… Sleepy…" She opened her mouth to yawn again, and he kissed her.

As soon as his lips touched hers, she melted.

Joel deepened his kiss, allowing his tongue to reach as far into her sweet mouth as he possibly could. He circled her tongue, taking his time to enjoy the flavor.

He could tell when her mood had changed. The mention of his aunt Sophie and the mean things she'd said had Samantha doing an about-face and running in the other direction.

He couldn't let that happen. Not after he realized what he felt for her.

He nibbled on her lower lip, sucking and pulling it into his mouth as he developed a strategy.

Her lips were luscious, juicy works of art, and they made for the perfect sweet and savory blend. Her mouth was a meal: dinner, dessert and a glass of fine wine. He could feast forever.

By now the recently yawning woman had her arms wrapped around his neck and did a slow and seductive grind against his pelvis as she picked up her pace and started to devour his mouth.

He'd bought himself some time. He had to keep kissing her.

She pulled away and ran her tongue across her lips. He felt a jolt from his gut to his groin. Forget making it hot, Samantha Dash sent him from sizzling to blazing. Her touch sent a scorching stream straight to his soul. He took her hand and led her to her bedroom.

They didn't say a word as he slowly undressed her. Her voluptuous body took his breath away. Each chocolate-covered curve begged to be touched, and he let his hand linger over them, one by one. He felt electric shocks as he caressed her skin. She must have felt them, too, because she shivered and moaned.

Naked, her full breasts called out for attention. The dark, tight nipples stood firm. He bent his head and took one in his mouth, suckling without a care in the world, still stroking her with his hands until they found the V between her legs. Without a moment of hesitation, he delved into the slick, wet folds of her womanhood, using his hands to bring pleasure he fully intended to heighten and heighten again as the night progressed.

By the time he was done with her, he didn't want there to be a doubt in her mind he was the only man for her. He didn't want any doubt they belonged together.

"Joel…" She reached up to try and take off his shirt.

He let the nipple he had been tasting pop out of his mouth. "Uh-uh. I got this. Just relax for a moment. Enjoy." He latched on to the other nipple.

"Mmm…but I want to touch you, too."

"We have all night long." He led her to the bed and placed her so he could devour each inch of delectable chocolate in his own pace.

Samantha felt as if she were going to scream. Joel seemed like a man on a mission, and the only thing she could do was accept each minute of his pleasure assault with mind-shattering orgasmic relish.

His lips knew how to spark desire, how to stoke it until it burst into flames, and those fire-starting lips were more than happy to tell all they knew to each spot on her body they kissed, suckled and nipped.

It all ended in her body feeling hot, satisfied and wanting more.

Even as he explored her with his mouth and hands, he remained fully clothed. She wanted to feel his skin against hers. She wanted to feel him filling her until she thought she might explode.

She wanted him, all of him.

By the time he got up from the bed and took off his clothes, she felt dizzy with pleasure.

Like a little kid who overdosed on sweets, she was high on his kisses and the orgasms his lips had brought her. The giddiness in her spread from her head to the tips of her toes, all she could do was look at him and smile a goofy smile.

His body. Lawd, his body was a sight to behold. Over six feet of brilliantly made, handsome, muscled steel. His pectorals offered perfection. His strong thighs were built for rides—slow, seductive rides and fast, wild rides. Any kind of ride a girl had in mind, and those thighs promised a smooth and exhilarating one.

He must have been reading her mind, because he put on their protection, got on the bed and laid down with two pillows under his head so that his back was slightly flexed.

Oh, yes, someone had been reading up on the best positions for men with chronic back pain.

He looked at her with a grin. "So you said you wanted to touch me. How about taking us both on a little ride?"

He didn't have to ask her twice.

She straddled him and allowed her already-soaking sex to envelop his manhood until their pelvises merged and he filled her to the hilt.

It felt so good. So damn good.

She had to give herself a minute to get used to the

way he stretched and completed her. When she started to move her hips, she closed her eyes.

"Look at me, sweetheart. Look at me and tell me what you see." His soft and firm command sent a sexy shiver through her body.

She opened her eyes and gazed at him. It was still there, all the devotion and caring she had seen earlier. Only this time it didn't make her want to run. It made her want to make her man feel good.

She rotated her hips, lifting up, spiraling back down, again and again, over and over. She moved like a woman possessed, loving the way he felt inside of her, teasing all of her spots as she angled her strokes.

She put her palms on his chest and moved her hips in a figure eight; *Cosmo girl*-style. At first she started slow. Then she rode him faster and faster. Samantha felt like she was going to explode.

She raised her arms above her head, arched her back. She loved the feel of her back. She loved the feel of her full breasts bouncing up and down, up and down. And judging from Joel's reaction—lust-filled eyes and groping hands squeezing her behind—so did he. Samantha rode him like a cowgirl, obsessed with how big and hot he felt inside of her.

She bent her head and licked his glistening stomach and chest letting her tongue trace a path to his mouth. She latched on, kissing him with all the emotions she felt inside. Even if she wasn't ready to verbalize the emotions he pulled out of her, she could make him feel it.

So she worked him. Steadily moving up and down. He met her thrust with slow steady, strokes of his own. He didn't have to do much to take her over the edge. She screamed her orgasm into his mouth with her eyes shut tight.

"Samantha, I love you." His words fell from his lips as he found his own release.

She opened her eyes and saw he had a tear falling down his cheek.

"What's wrong? Is it your back? I—" She quickly got off him. Her heart thumped with worry.

"No. My back is fine. I'm just happy. Content. Satisfied. Complete." He wrapped her in his arms and kissed her on her forehead.

Everything she could clearly see him feeling entered her heart and caused it to burst as her own eyes became damp with tears. She nodded. She felt the same.

Joel woke up the next morning feeling rejuvenated. For the first time in a long time he felt like he had a new lease on life—and was accepting his new journey, whatever it turned out to be.

He slipped on his shorts and walked into the living room. What he saw made him chuckle.

Samantha had her iPod on as she straightened up her apartment. She had on those jean shorts he loved and a cute pink T-shirt. She danced as she dusted and fluffed pillows.

Her hips swayed so nicely he could barely take his eyes off her. That wasn't what made him laugh. The picture she made swaying and cleaning was perfect. The sound? Well, that was another story.

His sweetheart might favor Jennifer Hudson in looks, but not in pipes. She sang along with Beyonce's "Upgrade U," and she was *way* off key.

"I can do for you what Martin did for the people. Ran by the men but the women keep the tempo… Let me upgrade you."

It sounded like coyotes baying at the moon.

So what, his perfect woman had a tiny little flaw? He watched her for a little bit longer until she started doing the shimmy and talking about ringing alarms.

She tossed a pillow in the air, spun around and caught it, as she did her little disco spin she saw him looking at her.

She jumped, and her eyes widened as she patted her chest. "Boy, you scared me half to death. How long were you standing there?" She took her earphones out and placed her hand on her hip.

"Long enough to watch your rendition of the oh-oh-oh-oh-oh-oh-oh-no-no. The dancing was hot, but…err…Beyonce called and said you can leave the singing to her. 'Crazy in Love' or not, you might wanna consider lip-synching." He chuckled at his own joke.

"Ooh… That's cold, and I was going to make you the most delicious brunch you've ever had. Now, I think I might let you starve."

"You'd starve a man for telling the truth? Okay, fine. You can sing your behind off. You should try out for *American Idol.* I'm sure Simon would love you." He laughed again.

She stood with her arms akimbo as she gave him a mock evil eye. "*Ha, ha…* How about you go shower and get dressed and when you get done, I'll feed you."

"That sounds like a plan. It would be even better if you could join me…."

"I showered over an hour ago, and I have to cook." She walked over and gave him a peck on the lips.

He licked his lips and turned to take a shower. Just as he did, he felt her give his behind a squeeze.

"Girl, don't start nothing you don't plan on finishing." He chuckled.

"Just testing the firmness." She squeezed again. She gave him a pat. "Now go shower." She giggled.

Torn between taking her on the sofa or dragging her in the shower with him, he decided to be good for now and bathe alone.

* * *

Samantha buzzed around her small galley kitchen trying to decide the best thing to cook. She wanted to impress him, but she didn't want to appear to be trying too hard.

So she settled for an egg-and-Swiss cheese casserole with lots of Swiss chard and some scallions chopped up in it. She also made some French toast on some nice thick, crusty bread she'd picked up from the bakery. After fresh-squeezing some orange juice and starting the coffee pot with some hazelnut flavored coffee, she decided she should check her messages quickly before Joel came back from his shower.

She pressed the button and tried to steel herself for the barrage to come. Her heart stopped when instead of hearing her mother's drunken slurred voice, she heard a man's voice she didn't recognize.

"Miss Dash, my name is Dr. Milford Corning and I'm calling about your mother, Mrs. Veronica Dash—" The rest of what he said got drowned out in her own ears, and all she could hear was her own scream.

Chapter 12

Joel hurried into the living room as soon as he heard Samantha's scream. Seeing her sitting on the couch, holding the phone and sobbing made his heart stop and his blood run cold. Without even knowing what was wrong, he knew without a doubt he would move mountains to bring a smile back to her face. He just hoped to God it was something he could help her with.

"Samantha, sweetheart, what's wrong? What happened?"

She glanced up at him with this vacant expression in her eyes. The tears were falling down her face in long, steady streams. Her lower lip quivered, and he felt sharp pain in his chest.

He sat down on the sofa next to her and put his arms around her. "Sweetheart, talk to me. Tell me what's wrong."

"My mother... I have to go to Chicago. Her doctor called. She's in the hospital, and they don't think she has much longer. They're only giving her a few more days... Her liver... The drinking... I should have..." She spoke in short, halting sentences and hiccupped through her tears.

"I should have known. I should have done something. Oh, my God, it's all my fault."

Joel couldn't fix this one for Samantha, but he could be there for her. He held her and rubbed her back, trying to think of words to say to console her in a situation that was inconsolable. His chest constricted and his heart felt heavy.

"It's not your fault, Samantha."

"It is. She started drinking really bad when my father was murdered. The few times I tried to talk to her about it, she reacted so negatively I just stopped bringing it up. A good daughter wouldn't have stopped. I should have gotten her some help."

He shook his head. It was clear now.

"In those kinds of situations folks have to want to help themselves." He held her tighter as he spoke, willing the words to settle and seep in so she could stop blaming herself.

She wiped her face with the back of her hand. "I'm sorry, Joel. Umm…you can eat the meal I prepared if you want. The food is done. I need to check on flights to Chicago. I hope I make it there in time." She gasped and chocked back her tears. "The doctor said she didn't have much time left…."

"How about you go and pack some things and I'll check on airline information for our trip to Chicago. I'll try and get us tickets for a flight this evening. We can head to the airport as soon as we stop by my place so I can pack up a few things."

"Joel, you don't have to go. You didn't know my mother—"

"But I know you, and there is no way I'm going to let you go through something like this alone."

There was no doubt in his mind, and he refused to hear any arguments. No one should be alone at a time like this, especially when they had people who loved them.

"That's asking a lot… I don't want to put you in that situation. You don't have to feel obligated just because we—"

He held up his hand, halting her speech. He knew where she was going, and he couldn't let her finish. Just because she hadn't realized what they had was real did not mean he could let her continue to only focus on the sexual nature of their relationship.

"I feel obligated because whether you acknowledge it or not, you're mine. Sweetheart, what part of 'I love you' do you not understand? I've got your back. You're not alone, not now, not ever again. You got that?" He stared into her tear-filled eyes until he was sure she, at least, heard him.

She started crying again and buried her head in his chest. He held her until the sobs tapered off.

He held her and kissed her forehead. "I'm going to start calling around for flights. Go pack a bag, sweetheart. Let's hurry and get you to your mother."

She didn't question him this time. She just got up and went to the bedroom.

He took the cordless phone and called several airlines before finally getting them tickets in first class for a flight out at 9:00 p.m. that evening.

Once they were on the plane to Chicago, she seemed to calm down a little, a few tears would run down her cheeks every so often, but she appeared to be all cried out for the moment.

And Joel, he finally knew what it meant to really love someone. Even though he had never met her mother, the fact Samantha was so distraught and he couldn't really do anything to change the situation broke his heart.

She rested her head on his shoulder.

"I want to thank you for coming with me, Joel. It means the world to me. You're such an amazing man. I'm… I'm just really glad to have you in my life."

He nodded. Telling her she didn't need to thank him because he loved her and would cut off his right arm if it would stop her pain didn't seem important. She still needed time to come to grips with the depths of his feelings for her, and that wasn't going to happen while she was worried about her mom.

He had booked them a hotel room near the hospital, and they stopped by the hospital directly from the airport. Her mother was in ICU and they had late visiting hours, but they only got a chance to peek in at her mother.

Veronica Dash was heavily sedated and out for the night. Her doctor spoke with them, and it didn't seem as if Samantha's mother had much longer. Joel only hoped the next morning wouldn't be too late for Samantha to see her mother and say good-bye.

As he held her in his arms when she finally drifted off to sleep, he prayed he would be able to offer her the support and comfort she would need to make it through this. There was nothing else more important to him at that moment.

The next morning, Samantha entered her mother's hospital room and stopped short just inside the door.

She stifled a gasp as she looked at her mother in the light of day. Even though she had peeked in on her the night before, nothing could have prepared her for seeing her mother with the sunshine brightening the stark, white hospital room.

Samantha's heart nearly beat its way out of her chest. The beating felt as if the organ was pushing its way past her chest cavity and splintering over and over again. She could feel new tears make their way down her face, and she forced herself to make baby steps forward. Each move felt like picking up a cement block and trying to drag it along.

She never thought she would see her mother like this.

Veronica Dash had been thin for years, ever since her husband's death. She had barely eaten anything for months after the murder, and years of drinking and a poor diet had turned the once full-figured mother Samantha knew as a child into the rail-thin woman she grew up knowing. However, none of that could have prepared her for the emaciated woman that lay in the hospital bed.

The disease had eaten away at the meat on Veronica's body. She was now just a skeleton with loose skin hanging off her.

Samantha couldn't stop the tears from streaming down her face. How did she let it get to this? She had just seen her mother eight months ago and she had been thin but fine.

The doctor said she had been diagnosed with cirrhosis of the liver a little under two years ago and told she needed to stop drinking if she wanted to be placed on a transplant list. She didn't do so and the cirrhosis gave way to cancer, which had spread throughout her body. And still, she kept drinking. It had gotten so bad that her body was deteriorating rapidly. The cancer had spread to most of her major organs, which were starting to shut down, and the doctor told Samantha it was only a matter of time.

Veronica had never even shared the news with Samantha.

Her mother opened her eyes and lifted her weak, thin hand to move the breathing mask that covered her mouth.

"Sammie... I knew you'd come before it was too late." Veronica's voice was raspy. She looked at Samantha with glazed-over eyes and it was hard to tell how lucid she was.

"Mom, I'm here. Oh, Mom... How could you let it get this bad? Why? Why didn't you tell me? Why didn't you stop?" She didn't even bother to wipe the tears from her face.

Joel placed his hand on her shoulder. "I'm going

to wait outside and let you two talk." Joel gave her shoulder a squeeze.

"No, you stay, young man." Veronica gazed up at Joel and then turned to Samantha. "Sammie, is this your boyfriend?"

She didn't know what to say. The hopeful look in her mother's eyes almost did her in.

"You're going to take care of my Sammie when I'm gone. I never really took care of her the way a mother should. She took care of me more than anything else. She needs someone to look out for her now like my sweet husband looked after me."

Samantha's gut twisted, and her heartbeat stalled.

"Yes, ma'am. I'll take care of Samantha for the rest of my days. You don't have to worry about her. She has me."

Samantha let out a breath and tried to calm herself. She'd have to apologize to Joel for her mother putting him on the spot.

Veronica gave a shaky smile. "That's good. He's a handsome one, Sammie. I see why you were so reluctant to come home more."

"No, Mom. If you had just told me you were sick, I would have been home on the first flight I could get. I would have come if you'd told me. Plus, we only met a few months ago."

If she had gotten a job in Chicago and moved

closer to home, she would have been there and seen the signs. She could have done something to prevent this. Her mother was dying, and it was all her fault. Her chest felt heavy, and a darkness set in so thick it threatened to choke her.

"I didn't want you to come just because I was sick. I wanted you to come because you wanted to come. Plus, when the doctors told me that I had cirrhosis of the liver a couple of years back, I knew I wasn't going to stop drinking." Veronica's face twisted slightly and she moved and contorted as if her body had a mind of its own.

Samantha thought she saw a glimpse of the guilt in her mother's eyes at her confession.

"Without anything to numb me, the pain of losing your father is just too much. Honestly, I wanted to die then but I told myself I had to stay alive for you. You probably would have been better off if I had—"

Her voice sounded so frail, and her body seemed to struggle with each word. Samantha had to stop her. She needed to save her strength. And none of the past mattered now.

"Don't say that, Mom. That's not true. I needed you. I loved you. I'm so sorry I didn't try harder to get you to stop drinking. If I had moved back home after graduate school, maybe I could have… Oh,

Mom, I don't want you to die." She choked out her words—words that felt inadequate, words that would never right the wrongs.

"It's okay, Sammie. I'm at peace with it. At least there'll be no more pain, and if God isn't too peeved with me for being a drunk and a bad mother, maybe I'll get to be in heaven with your daddy. I sure hope so." She lifted her hand and tried to put the breathing mask back on.

Samantha reached over and secured the mask for her mother.

"Are you okay? Should we get a nurse?" Joel asked.

Veronica feebly nodded her head slowly.

Joel rushed out of the room to get help.

Samantha placed her hand on her mother's shoulder and prayed. She wasn't ready to say good-bye. A daughter is never ready.

It wasn't fair. She had really lost both parents when she was twelve. The woman who drank her life away was a ghost of the woman she used to know, but that ghost was the only mother she had.

"I love you, Mom. I've always loved you. Please don't leave me." Samantha sobbed out her words and willed her mother to live.

Veronica looked at her, and Samantha could have sworn she saw a smile in her eyes before they glazed over into nothingness.

Her wail assaulted the air at the same time that her mother flat-lined.

By the time Joel made it back with the doctor and nurse, Veronica Dash had passed away. The doctor simply called the time of death since her mother had requested not to be resuscitated.

Samantha's heart broke in so many pieces she didn't know how she would put them back together or if she even wanted to.

Chapter 13

Samantha called the clinic to let her supervisor, Lisa Howard, know that she would need a little time off from work to bury her mother and wrap up her mother's affairs.

"Girl, first let me say that I'm so sorry to hear about your mom. I'm so sorry. That has to be the worst feeling in the world. I'll keep you in my thoughts and prayers." Jenny paused and sighed.

"Are you sitting down? I have something to tell you before I transfer you to Lisa." Jenny spoke in a hushed whisper.

Samantha sat down on the hotel bed. She hoped

nothing had happened to Jenny's kids or her husband, Walt.

"I'm sitting down. What happened?"

"Some woman called the clinic Monday wanting to speak to whoever was in charge. Something told me to find out more about what she wanted first before connecting her with Lisa, but I didn't follow my first mind." Jenny stopped and Samantha could almost see her friend's facial expressions and her bouncing in her seat. She always bounced when she got excited or antsy. "Dang, I should have followed my first mind! Anyway, I just connected her and come to find out she called to complain about you."

Her mouth dropped open and her eyes went wide. "Me? Was she a former patient? Why would she complain about me? What did Lisa say?"

Samantha knew she was always the consummate professional with her patients. She did her job well, and for the most part had a nice and easy rapport with all of her patients.

"Lisa said the woman went on and on about you being a slut who seduced patients and that you were currently having an affair with at least one of your patients, maybe more. The woman suggested you might be using the clinic as a clandestine massage parlor to find unsuspecting johns for your prostitution ring. Lisa said the woman just had a million and one ways to call you a whore, basically."

Sophie!

She thought back to the Hightower family cookout and the harsh words Joel's aunt had spoken. If she were a betting woman, she would put her money on Sophie.

Now in addition to burying her mother she had to worry about having a job when she got back to New Jersey. She might even have to worry about going to jail, because if the old woman had cost her a job, she couldn't say for sure she wouldn't snap and break Sophie's evil, hateful neck.

"Just transfer me to Lisa so I can tell her I'll be in Chicago, burying my mother and settling her affairs." She didn't even feel like discussing Sophie anymore.

She wanted to tell Jenny dating Joel had been a bad idea after all. But thinking of the way he had been there for her from the moment she found out about her mother and each step of the way after, the way he was still with her, helping her with arrangements and holding her when it just became too much to bear, she knew deciding to give their attraction a chance to grow into something more had been the best decision she'd made in a long time.

He had become her rock, her protector, her safe harbor. There was no way she could give him up.

Even if her boss demanded it, she couldn't. The ache in her chest would be too painful if she lost him.

She realized she had fallen in love with Joel Hightower.

She'd fallen in love with a man who could possibly go back to a dangerous job and put her at risk of mourning him the way her mother had mourned her father.

When Lisa came on the line, her supervisor expressed her condolences and then gave the streamlined and sanitized version of what the complaining caller said.

Samantha didn't miss a beat. She was in love, and life, sweet precious life, was too short.

"Lisa, I just want to say I have started dating a patient. We were attracted to one another from the beginning and I did nothing about it for the first two-and-a-half months because of my professionalism and the fact I do value my position at the clinic. Unfortunately, love refuses to be put on hold or follow protocol, and I'm glad, because he has been the only thing between me and unbearable grief right now. It's not a shady affair. I've found the man I love."

She had no idea what made her blurt out her confession to her boss before she even told her man, but there was something about knowing it that made her want to scream it from the rooftops, go tell it on the mountain and sing it to the world. She loved Joel and he loved her.

Joel Hightower was the only man for her, and it was about time she admitted it to herself and to him. He'd already confessed his love. She hadn't wanted to believe it when he said it, but his actions the past couple of days showed her the truth.

"Samantha, we'll still have to have a formal hearing with you when you get back to discuss the complaints of prostitution and your relationship with this patient. We just need to check into things and make sure the complaint is unfounded. We all know you, Samantha, and we know you wouldn't do anything to jeopardize your career or the clinic, and I for one, couldn't be happier that you've fallen in love."

Samantha could almost feel Lisa's smile from across the phone lines. She expelled a breath she didn't even know she'd been holding.

"I'll try and get back as soon as possible, Lisa."

"Take your time. Losing your mother is hard. I'm glad you have someone to help you through it," Lisa said.

Samantha felt the tears running down her face.

She was glad, too.

When Joel came back to the hotel room with breakfast, he found Samantha sitting on the bed with the cell phone in her hands, crying.

Placing the bagels and coffee on the small corner table, he went to her immediately and held her.

"We need to head out to the funeral home to tie up the details for the wake and funeral, sweetheart."

He hated bringing it up, but they had a lot of ground to cover. Since Samantha was an only child, there were no other immediate family members left to handle the planning. Her mother had pretty much alienated anyone else.

It made him all the more glad he had insisted he make this trip with her.

She wiped her face. "Someone called my job and made a complaint against me."

He couldn't hold back the angry twitch in his jaw when she relayed all the things someone had called her job and said about her.

Aunt Sophie had gone too far this time. He was going to put an end to her reign of terror as soon as he got back to New Jersey.

"You're a stellar physical therapist. You're professional, and most important, you really didn't stand a chance of resisting me once I put my game down. I was determined to have you. You had no choice but to give in." He rubbed her back as he spoke and tried to keep the smile out of his voice.

She pulled away and crossed her arms over her chest.

He kept a straight face.

"What? You know you wanted me from the first moment you set eyes on me. I think it's commendable you wanted to hold on to your ideals and all that, but it was really an exercise in futility. Not only am I irresistible, but I always get my girl."

He made a show of shrugging nonchalantly.

She smiled. "You are *sooo* modest. It amazes me how a guy that is as awesome as you are can be *sooo* humble."

"I know, right? I blow my own mind with how low-key and understated my swagger is." He brushed off his shoulder for show. "To be fair, I'm not irresistible to the entire female population—"

"No!" she interrupted in mock horror.

"Yes. Shocking, isn't it? But actually, there is really only one woman whose tolerance and resistance levels turn to mush when I'm around, and lucky woman that you are, it's you." He brushed her lips with a kiss. "Don't faint now. I know what my touch does to you."

Her smile widened, and she shook her head.

Seeing her smile lifted his spirit. "I love you, sweetheart. I love you more than words could express, and I'm dedicated to making you happy and making you smile."

She giggled softly. "Thanks. I needed that."

"I know. Now go clean up those tear tracks so we can get moving."

She saluted and offered, "Yes, sir," in a sassy voice.

Smiling, he teased, "I think I can get used to that kind of obedience."

He chuckled when her lips twisted to the side.

Lightly tapping her bottom, he said, "Get a move on, Little Miss Spitfire."

All through the wake, the funeral and cleaning out her mother's home, Samantha saw she could count on Joel in ways she would never have imagined.

When they got to her parents' bedroom, she found both of her parents' things in the closets and dresser drawers. Even though she'd known her mother had never gotten rid of her father's things, seeing them there the way they must have looked the day he died sent a sharp pain through her chest.

And here she was, setting herself up for the same downfall if Joel got clearance to return to his dangerous job.

She could lose him, and it would probably kill her, too.

The realization hit her like a fist to the gut because it meant she had made the ultimate mistake. Not only she had fallen head over heels in love with Joel

Hightower, but she had risked more than her heart in the process.

Was she really stronger than her mother in that regard? She liked to tell herself throughout the years she would have done a better job coping for her children if she'd been in her mother's shoes, but that was easy to say when she hadn't been deep in love.

As her tears began a steady trail down her face, she felt strong arms enclose her in an embrace.

"Let me hire someone to do at least this room for you, sweetheart. I know it must be hard."

She could feel Joel's soft breath on the base of her neck as he spoke.

It was too late to save her heart or play it safe. If she gave him up now, she would be heartbroken. If she stayed with him and he died performing his dangerous job, she would be devastated, as well. No matter how she cut it, loving a man in a dangerous job could destroy her the way it had destroyed her mother.

"No. I need to do this." She took a deep, calming breath. "I can't believe she never gave away his things. It's like she never recovered from the loss because she never really let go."

He didn't say anything. He just held her close.

"I don't want to be that vulnerable to heartache. I'm terrified of ending up like her." Her words came out in such a hushed whisper she could barely hear herself, and it was too late to wonder if he'd heard her. She felt his body go still.

He had heard her.

She pulled away and turned to him. "I'm going to get started in here. The sooner we get done here the sooner we can head back to Jersey and find out the fate of my job."

It took everything in him not to pull her back into his arms and make her believe her heart was safe with him. He understood her hesitation. His father's words about why he had started Hightower Security came to mind and made him question his own situation and his own desires to go back to a job he loved.

Would he lose Samantha if he were allowed to go back to firefighting? Would it be asking too much of her to ask her to remain with him despite her history, pain and fears? Could he look at her each day and know his job added to her worry and stress? Could he leave a job he loved to give the woman who had captured his heart her peace of mind?

At the end of the day, which of his loves would win out and which would be sacrificed for the other? He had no idea how to answer any of those questions. The only thing he knew for certain was that after finding this incredible woman to love, he didn't want to ever let her go.

* * *

When they made it back to New Jersey, after weathering her mom's death together, Samantha knew without a doubt they could probably make it through anything. That's why she knew she had to go and face his aunt Sophie one-on-one to clear the air and try to get an understanding of why she felt the need to do what she did.

Joel came with her to Sophie's place but she told him that she wanted and needed to face Sophie alone. He agreed to wait downstairs in her senior complex just in case. Him coming to the complex actually worked out well because she needed his voice to get Sophie to buzz them into the building. The woman probably wouldn't have buzzed her up.

The look on Sophie's face when she opened the door and saw Samantha there instead of her beloved nephew gave *nasty* a new meaning.

Samantha didn't wait for an invitation and instead just pushed her way into the apartment.

"So, tell me, Sophie, what exactly did I do to you to make you think it would be fun to try to ruin my career?"

Sophie let the door slam.

"Where's my nephew? I buzzed him up, not you. Should I call security?" Sophie folded her arms across her chest and glared at Samantha.

"You could. I can't stop you, but I was hoping that since you were woman enough to call my place of employment and complain about me—albeit a cowardly anonymous call—that you would be woman enough to have a civil conversation about why you did it." It was all she could do to hold her own hands at her sides and not slap them upside Sophie's head.

"You don't have any proof that I did anything."

"You do realize that our offices have caller ID? And we could easily get the phone records to see where incoming calls on that day came from." She smirked when she said it and hoped that she exuded an air of confidence because they did not have caller ID and there was no way she could really prove Sophie did it.

She just knew Sophie had done it.

"I—I—I… Well…listen, I didn't call your job, but *if* I did, I didn't do anything wrong. I'm sure it's against the rules for you to date your patients."

Mmm…hmm…stuttering and *lying*.

"Actually, it's not against the rules, and it's your accusation of prostitution that was the big issue." Samantha rolled her eyes in disgust. "Why would you do that? What did I do to you besides date and fall in love with your nephew. *I love him,* and you are trying to sully our relationship with your innuendo and malicious behavior."

"Can we sit down and have this talk? My legs aren't what they used to be." Sophie's shoulders seemed to sag a little as she dropped her arms to her sides.

She followed Sophie to the living room and sat down. For the first time since she'd met the woman, Sophie actually looked sorry.

They took seats on Sophie's pink-and-green floral Queen Anne furniture, and Samantha made sure she held Sophie's gaze. After several minutes, Sophie looked away.

"I'm sorry," Sophie mumbled.

Samantha squinted but kept looking at Sophie. "What? I didn't hear you."

"I'm sorry! For what it's worth, it wasn't about you, really. You actually seem like a decent girl, unlike that gutter trash Penny and that common sister-in-law of mine. In fact, if Celia didn't like you so much, I might not have been so against you, but she did like you, and that made you my enemy."

Incredulous and stunned beyond belief, Samantha opened her mouth and closed it again several times before responding.

"This is crazy. Why do you hate your sister-in-law so much? What did she do to you to make you want to make everyone miserable?"

"She's a backstabbing slut who used her relation-ship with me to snag herself a man of stature, a Hightower." Sophie sat up straight in her chair then and her eyes took on a hateful glare.

"She was a little nothing in the street who I tried to mentor as a part of my sorority's outreach program many years ago. I encouraged her to go to college and exposed her to the finer qualities of life, and she repaid me by causing my only brother, my baby brother, to marry beneath himself."

Samantha blinked. She could hear the hurt in Sophie's voice and she could tell the woman thought she really had legitimate reasons for terrorizing people. She could also tell the woman needed more help than she could ever give her.

"From what I can tell, Celia Hightower is a good woman. She's sweet and treats everyone with kindness." *She tolerated your hatefulness for years, so that makes her a saint in my book.*

Samantha took a deep breath. "I really hope that your misplaced grudge hasn't cost me my career. I sacrificed a lot to get to where I am today." She thought about her relationship with her mother and bit back her tears. Taking a deep breath, she willed herself to be strong.

"But I can tell you what I won't sacrifice—my feelings for Joel. That man is the best thing to ever happen to me, and I intend to remain a part of his life, job or no job."

She had to shake her head and grin at that one, as much as she had been touting professionalism a few months ago, she would have never thought she would reach a point where she could even utter the words, *job or no job*.

"Are you finished, young lady?" Sophie reared up in her seat as if she had the right to be indignant.

And Samantha had to bring her back down.

"No! I am not! But I only have a few more things to add. I just lost my mother, and thanks to you, I may very well lose my job. If that happens, I can't promise that I won't *totally* lose it and come looking for you." She paused for effect. "What *you* need to do is stay as far away from me as you can. I'm not Celia. I don't have her patience or her grace—"

"*Celia* and *grace* shouldn't even be mentioned in the same sentence. Anyway, you don't have to worry about me coming around. That *woman*—and I use the word loosely—has finally managed to turn my brother against me and I am no longer welcome in their home—a home I grew up in, my family home, all because I'm the only one who doesn't hold her tongue and says what needs to be said."

"You just don't get it, do you?" Samantha eyed Sophie incredulously. "Life is too short to carry around this kind of negativity. You need to let all that stuff go. Do you want to die bitter and alone because you've run your family away? My mother…" She closed her eyes and cursed as the tears started to fall.

She thought of her weak mother lying in the hospital bed and her horrendous death. She opened her eyes and wiped the tears away. At least she had made it back so that her mother's last minutes weren't alone.

She looked at Sophie and she thought she saw a hint of kindness in her eyes.

"For what it's worth, I'm sorry to hear about your mother. I hear she died from complications due to alcoholism. Is that true?"

Samantha arched her right eyebrow.

Lord. Give. Me. Strength.

"Because those kinds of addictions tend to be genetic…" Sophie studied her and gave one of her snobbish sniffs.

Samantha tilted her head and leaned forward. "I don't drink."

"And you shouldn't, given your family history. I'm thinking about the implications if, God forbid, my nephew decides to marry you and you have children. We really can't have future Hightowers running around here with such high potential for chemical addictions. I mean, really… Penny's mother, Carla, was a former crack addict, your mother was an alcoholic… You're a smart girl. You can see why I worry. I'm not doing this to be mean or hateful. I'm thinking about my family's legacy—a legacy that depends on the women that the men in this family choose to wed… Trust me, we lucked out that I was there to help out with Patrick, Lawrence, Joel and Jason. I won't be here for the next generation."

If she hadn't just come back from burying her mother, she would have thanked the Lord that Sophie wouldn't be around for the next generation, but no matter how much the woman tested her Christianity, she was not going to let Sophie High-tower take her there.

"You know what, Sophie? I'm gonna pray for you." Samantha got up and started walking toward the door.

"Pray for me? I go to church every Sunday. I'm the head of the deaconess board at Mt. Zion Baptist." There was no holding back Sophie's indignation now.

"Mmm, hmm. So, I guess you missed the part about not bearing false witness and not lying in the Ten Commandments? I'm going to pray that you start living the word you get every Sunday in church." She turned and looked Sophie up and down before opening the door. "Stay blessed." She let herself out.

When she got downstairs, Joel was waiting for her in the lobby. Seeing him and knowing he had her back let her know that she could face anything the future brought, even a million Aunt Sophies. Joel and the love she felt for him made everything worthwhile and right. Even finally letting go of the fear that his dangerous job might cause her to lose him in the future. None of that mattered when she factored in the love they felt for one another.

"I was about to come up there and check on you." Joel wrapped her in his strong arms and planted a loving kiss on her lips. "How did it go?"

"It went like it went. I do realize that your aunt has more issues than I could ever hope to combat, and I also realize how your mother tolerated her for so long." She smiled as she noted the puzzled expression that crossed his face.

"Really? Well, you can fill me in on that one, because I honestly have no clue."

"Celia isn't going to let that woman steal her joy or stop her from having the man she loved, and neither am I."

Chapter 14

"So, you're saying I won't be able to go back to work fighting fires?"

The doctors—both the fire department's representative, Dr. Moore, and his own, Dr. Lardner—sat across from Joel after an extensive exam, bearing news he didn't want to hear.

"The damage to your spine was extensive, and while your surgeries and therapy worked to greatly increase your quality of life, I'm afraid I can't recommend that you return to the fire department in the same capacity, no. You need a stronger, healthier back to even wear the heavy uniform required. Not to mention the lifting that you'd have to do in the job. Your back just isn't there yet, and frankly, I'm not sure it ever will be there again." Dr. Moore looked him in the eyes and kept his stare firm.

"Quality of life! Are you kidding me? What kind of quality of life will I have if I can't go back to work?" Joel bit his words out angrily.

This was unbelievable, all the hard work, all the hopes and prayers, for what? Nothing. What a rip-off. He glared at Dr. Lardner. "You said if I worked hard, there might be a chance!"

"I said there *might* be. Joel, you do have a chance at a normal life without severe handicap. Do you realize how many—" Dr. Lardner started.

"I want my life back!" Joel pounded his fist on the table.

Didn't they understand? It was like they were telling him he wasn't good enough. That he was no longer man enough...

Maybe he wasn't. He shook his head. He needed air.

He felt tears of anger moisten his eyes.

Great!

All he needed to make the total loss of his masculinity complete was to start bawling like a baby, but that was how he felt. Just like a neglected child crying out for help.

When you've done everything you were supposed to do and can't get what you want, then what?

"What am I supposed to do now?" His voice didn't even sound the same to his ears. It sounded weak, and it made him even angrier.

"Joel, you can still work for the fire department. You can work in investigation, forensics—" Dr. Moore started.

"I don't want a desk job. I want my life back…." His words filtered off as he realized he had said that already. He'd said it and had gotten no response. It wasn't going to happen.

He felt like screaming, but it wouldn't have done a bit of good.

"Just forget it, Docs. Sorry for wasting your time."

He got into his car and drove until he couldn't drive any more, and then he ended up at his old firehouse. He sat outside, watching the building for longer than he would have ever admitted to anyone.

He remembered what it used to feel like—the rush, the desire to help others, the adrenaline, the thrill. It took everything in him not to break down and cry.

Suspended.

Well, at least it was with pay. That was the only bright side of an increasingly gloomy situation. Until Samantha's supervisor's investigated the complaints of prostitution made against her, Samantha would still be able to get a paycheck. She had no worries that they would find any evidence of prostitution. It just stung her Sophie had been able to cause so much havoc. At least she still had her job, though.

Thank God for small favors. She had no idea how she would have reacted to coming back from burying her mother and finding out the glorious job she had loved and had used as an excuse not to move back to Chicago when her mother was alive was no longer hers.

And then there were her feelings for Joel. The same Joel who was meeting with his doctors to find out if his back had healed enough for him to go back to work. Between the fate of her own career and his career, in a sense their entire relationship was hanging in the balance.

It was all she could do not to yank her hair out at the roots. Lord knows she'd been tugging and pulling at her twists with worry and angst all afternoon.

Joel was supposed to have been here hours ago. The only thing she could think was he'd found out he could return to the fire department and went out celebrating with his firemen friends. She practiced smiling and looking happy while she waited. Would she be able to smile and say, "Baby, that's wonderful," if he came in with news his doctors had given him the okay to go back to work?

In her opinion, it would be a mistake for him to go back in the same capacity he had been serving. The heavy uniform alone would tax his back beyond its limits, and God forbid if he had to carry anyone out of a fire, but she couldn't tell if that was Samantha the girlfriend's or Samantha the physical therapist's opinion.

This is why one should not date one's patients, she chastised herself. *Oh, well, too late to worry about that now. The lines are forever blurred where Joel Hightower is concerned.*

The knock on the door broke her out of her reverie. When she answered it, she found Joel standing there. She hoped she would be able to be the kind of woman he deserved after the way he stood by her side. She prayed that God gave her the strength to stand by her man, dangerous job and all.

After driving around for hours, he ended where he was supposed to be. The only thing was, the news he'd gotten this afternoon made him question if he was *really* supposed to be there. What kind of man would he be for her now? What kind of life could he give her?

"Hey…you." Samantha studied him carefully as he entered her apartment.

He could tell by her careful gaze she must have been worried about him.

"Hey, sweetheart." He couldn't help it. He had to touch her, so he pulled her into his arms and hugged her.

Big mistake. How was he supposed to let her go now?

He followed her into her living room.

"Well, my doctor said my back has improved immensely, and I know I owe that all to you."

"No. You did the work. I'm proud of you."

"Thanks, but even with all that work, I'm still not going to be able to return to firefighting, at least not in the capacity that I'm used to. They offered me a chance to train and take the test for the inspection division, a desk job." He might as well go work for his father. He would do that before he took a desk job with the fire department.

"That could be nice. You'd be able to help with things like arson, and I know it's not what you wanted to hear, baby, but…"

"You don't get it. This back problem has stolen everything from me. I feel like half a man, and you don't need half a man. So maybe we should quit this while we're ahead."

She frowned and stared at him for a minute before shaking her head.

His eyes started to glaze over, and he again willed himself to hold it together. No matter how low he felt, he didn't want to leave her with the image of him breaking down.

"What do you mean 'quit this while we're ahead?'" She placed her hands on her hips and struck the black woman akimbo battle pose.

"I'm saying you deserve better and I have to be man enough to let you go so you can have it." His shoulders slouched, and he didn't even try to straighten them.

The heaviness in his head as he tried to grapple with the loss of his job and the heaviness in his heart as he tried to man up and let Samantha go wouldn't allow for straight-back postures or cool poses. His form reflected how he felt. There was nothing he could do about it.

"I'm sorry, sweetheart. I thought I'd be getting my job back and I'd be able to be the man you deserve—" he started.

"I. Know. You. Didn't." The pain and anger in her voice chilled him to the bone. "I know you didn't just sit in my living room, after making me fall in love with your behind and tell me we should just quit this. Did the doctors give you some crazy dust or something with their diagnosis? Because you must have lost your mind, coming in here running this foolishness by me."

"I can't even make love to you the way I want to. I can't—"

She cut him off with a quickness and a roll of the neck for good measure. "Do you see me complaining? You're the best lover I've ever had and have blown my mind and stolen my heart, you idiot! And if your job as a fireman is that important to you, then I will work with you until your back is strong enough for you to go back."

"Idiot? Hey, that's not nice—"

"Well, as you have been fond of telling me, *I ain't nothing nice!* I have to keep it real with you, and on the real, you have my heart. You can't just throw it back at me without a good cussing out."

Tears started to fall down her cheeks. He remembered what his father said about not being able to take his mother's tears. If his father felt even a tenth of what he felt like seeing Samantha cry, then he knew why his father felt that way. He couldn't bear to see the moisture pool in her beautiful brown eyes and then flow down her lovely face. And knowing that she was crying because of him made it all the worse.

He wrapped his arms around her, and she pushed him away.

"Don't cry, sweetheart. Please. I'm sorry. You're right. I'm an idiot. Just don't cry. It breaks my heart." Suddenly the pain that he felt about not being able to fight fires moved to the background. While he still felt hurt, he really wanted to do what he could to make things right for Samantha. That meant more than anything else.

That was love.

"Good. You should be feeling what I'm feeling right now. Do you know I've been sitting here for hours waiting for you and practicing how I was going to look happy for you when you told me you were going back to your dangerous job?" She choked her words out in a sob. "Even though it would probably kill me if something were to happen to you, I would be willing to risk it because I love you and I want you happy."

He pulled her into his arms and kissed away her tears. "I'm sorry." He covered her mouth and felt a clarity he hadn't felt in months.

He hadn't fought a fire in ages, but he'd had all the fire and passion a man's heart could stand for the past three months.

She kissed him back aggressively. It was as if she was placing everything she felt in the kiss.

He led her back into the bedroom and stood in awe as she literally ripped off his clothes. Her passion invigorated him, and he found himself ripping off her clothing, as well. He grabbed a condom before they tumbled to the bed and he crept up behind her. He placed his hands on the bed on either side of her and slightly flexed his upper torso over her back. He slowly entered the slick welcoming heat of her womanhood.

* * *

Samantha couldn't stifle the moan as Joel filled her. How could he even question how he made her feel? And how dare he try and take this away from her after showing her what making love with her heart fully involved felt like?

She moved her hips back slowly, savoring the thick length of his manhood as he stroked her steadily, with strength unparalleled. She moved forward then back, forward then back; hips undulating, rocking and going in circles.

Oh, yes.

"I'm sorry, sweetheart. Please forgive me." He trailed soft kisses down her back.

Each power-filled stroke after that sent her spiraling closer and closer to splendor. Every place on her body seemed to tighten until she thought she would explode, and then it happened.

"Baby, I'm so, so sorry… I love you." Joel's words pierced her soul and blocked out all her pain, fear and doubt.

"Ohh…Joel!"

"Yes, sweetheart. I love you so much. Come for me, baby."

He reached his arm around to her front and flicked the bud in her dripping center back and forth. Gently twisting and rubbing it in circles.

"Come for me, Samantha. You know you want to."

She felt her sex squeeze and pull at him as if it were grasping for its last meal. She tightened and tightened over and over until she heard Joel scream out.

"I love you, sweetheart."

"I love you, too."

As she waited for Joel to come back from getting rid of the protection, she tried to get a hold of her emotions.

He was actually going to break up with her over nonsense.

Calm down, girl. He came to his senses.

He walked back into the bedroom and sat on the bed. "So, you finally realized that you love a brother, huh?"

He had that sexy little smile on his face and that devilish and playful gleam in his eyes.

She shook her head and crossed her arms across her chest.

Oh, no, Hightower, you're going to have to come with more than the I'm-so-charming-and-irresistible routine.

"So what if I do love you? You're willing to throw it all away because of some misguided notion you have about…what exactly, Joel? I mean, I'm your physical therapist. I knew what your back problems were when I got involved with you, against my better judgment, and I put my career and my heart on the line, for what?"

He leaned over and kissed her. She gobbled up each stroke of his tongue, each caress of his lips and moaned for more.

But it won't be that easy, either, baby boy....

She pulled away. "So, if you want to leave me, leave."

"I don't want to leave you. I want to marry you. I want to make you my wife, and I want you to be the mother of my children."

Well, now that might work....

"So, will you?" He had a pleading expression on his face and that loving gleam in his eyes.

"Will I what?"

"Will you marry me? I realize you mean more to me than fighting fires. Sweetheart, please say yes."

"Okay, yes."

He kissed her, softly, gently.

"You know, I think I fell in love with you the first time I saw you, too, before I even got to know you, when you were lying in the hospital emergency room and they were flashing that handsome heroic grill of yours all over the news. I made up this sweet, sexy, funny, caring guy to go with that picture, and I fell in love with him, and even though it took a long time after we met for that guy to surface, I still loved him. He really is you, and I love you…so much…."

Her heart twisted as she got the words out, but she

really wanted him to know what he was about to give up.

"I love you and it doesn't matter to me what you do for a living. You can be a fireman, a fire investigator, an employee at Hightower Security. The only thing I see that matters when I look at you is that you are my man, and you are all the man I will ever need." She stared him in the eye so that he got it.

A tear slid down his cheek and he nodded. "I want to get married as soon as possible."

"Oh, I don't know about that, baby boy. I'm thinking a nice long engagement so that you can prove you're really sure about this—that you really want a spitfire for a wife. Because I can't promise I won't light fire to you with my mouth if you come in here talking that kind of foolishness again."

"Since you took my surly heart and gave me back my joy, I'm more than willing to wait for you. You make it hot, sweetheart. You make life worth living."

"And you better never forget it. I love you, Joel."

"I love you, too, sweetheart. I love you, too."

Epilogue

Getting all of the Hightower brothers together once a week was becoming increasingly difficult with two of the brothers having met their soul mates, but somehow, they had managed to get together for happy hour at the sports bar in downtown Paterson after a couple of months of hit-or-miss meetings.

Joel had been busy getting used to his new position as the new VP in charge of the Home Safety Division of Hightower Security, and he found that the proactive work he did in his new job to make sure that people were able to secure their homes filled the need he had as a fireman to help others in a different but still very satisfying way. Samantha's suspension was lifted after two weeks of paid leave when the investigation committee found that the claims of the anonymous caller were unfounded, and his new fiancée showed him every day that he was all the man she needed. The thrill and rush he got from being with her still sparked his desire, and he didn't see that ending anytime soon. Everything he used to get from his old job as a fireman was still present in his life in abundance. He felt happy as he joined his brothers, happy and just fine with his life.

Joel walked up to the booth and slid in. He was the last to arrive, but he had a good excuse—at least it was a good excuse to him. He and Samantha had finally settled on a date to get married. She had made him sweat for it and work for it, no doubt, but it was all worth it, and some of the work had actually been fun.

"Look who decided to show up, the other love-bird," Patrick held up his drink in mock salute. "There are only two of us left to hold down the fort, and since I've been down that road before, I can tell you, I won't be going back."

"And you know my motto, if she can't burn in the kitchen like Mama, she need not apply." Lawrence raised his glass, and he and Patrick toasted.

Jason laughed. "It's going to be so funny to watch love take the two of you out."

"You forget, baby bro, I mastered the game. I'm

not only a client, I'm the player president." Lawrence dusted off his collar and winked.

Joel shook his head. "All right, I have great news to share."

"Me, too," Jason added.

Joel looked at his youngest brother. If the news was what he thought it was, then this was going to be a night of celebration indeed.

"Penny is pregnant. I'm going to be a dad. We've known for the past three months, but we wanted to wait, you know, to make it past the first trimester before we shared the news." Jason's eyes gleamed with excitement.

"That's wonderful. I can't wait to be an uncle." Lawrence put all his joking aside.

Patrick stood and embraced, Jason. "Congratulations, baby bro. This is amazing news. Give Penny a hug for me."

It was hard not to get a little choked up knowing about how Penny and Jason lost their first child to a miscarriage when they were high-school sweethearts. They had spent fifteen years apart, and God saw fit to give them another chance.

The brothers all stood and gave each other hugs and love and then settled back into their seats.

"Samantha has agreed to set a date. We've started planning our fall wedding. So, you clowns are going to have to get dressed up in those tuxedos and dust off your electric slide, because come October, the High-towers are going to have another wedding to celebrate."

"That's wonderful, man. She's a great woman," Jason offered.

"And she can cook her behind off," Lawrence added. "Hey, should we order some Buffalo wings or something?"

"Your mind stays on food. It's a wonder you stay in shape at all." Patrick shook his head at Lawrence. He turned to Joel. "Samantha seems like a nice girl. I'm happy for you, bro."

"Let's toast then." Jason held up his glass. "To every Hightower finding the love of his life—"

Patrick put his glass down. "Nah, buddy, I can't toast to that there. I'm going to have to pass."

Lawrence put his glass down, too. "No need to tempt fate. I like being single." He stared across the room.

Jason followed his gaze and so did Joel.

"Isn't that the McKnight twins? They just got back out of prison. Do you think they're up to any trouble tonight?" Jason turned back to look at Lawrence.

"Who's that little sexy girl with them? She looks like a young Jada Pinkett-Smith from her pre-Will, *A Different World* days. She's a hottie. What is she doing with thugs like those?" Jason asked.

Patrick shook his head. "You see, that's why I

won't drink to that 'Hightowers finding love' stuff. Finding a woman with some sense and who's about something is next to impossible."

Jason laughed. "She looks like a young Jada, all right, but if she's hanging with the McKnight Twins, you better make that Jada from *Set It Off*."

"Do you know her?" Joel asked Lawrence.

Lawrence just kept staring at the group.

Patrick nudged Lawrence's shoulder.

"Huh?" Lawrence gave them an irritated glare. "What?"

"Joel asked you if you knew her, the girl with the McKnights. She looks kind of young—"

"I don't know her, but I intend to keep an eye on her." Lawrence spoke the words and planted his gaze back on the young woman.

But they had too much to celebrate tonight to give it too much thought. He was going to be an uncle and his sweetheart was going to bless him by becoming his wife.

He'd come to think of the accident as not the end of life as he'd known it, but the beginning of a life more rich and fulfilling than he ever could have imagined. His little spitfire had brought the joy, passion and heat back into his life and he could only see things getting better from there.

"So, let's toast to finding happiness, then, because I have found mine." He held his glass up.

"I'll drink to that, because I've found mine, too."
Jason grinned.

"I guess I can drink to that, even though I think
happiness is way overrated, and it's fleeting. The
wrong woman can ruin a man's happiness for the rest
of his life—"

"All right, all right, just toast, grouch." Jason cut
Patrick off.

Joel saw Lawrence was still paying close attention
to the young woman with the McKnights. He kicked
Lawrence under the table.

"Ouch! What?" Lawrence snapped as he kept
watching the young woman.

"We're toasting to finding happiness," Jason offered.

"Yeah, yeah, to finding happiness." Lawrence
lifted his glass and all the while kept his focus in the
McKnights' direction. "I'll be right back." He got up
and walked over there.

"What's that about?" Patrick asked.

"Damn if I know." Jason shrugged.

"Finding happiness?" Joel glanced back at the
young woman who had apparently captured his
brother's attention. She looked like a no-nonsense kind
of sister. Maybe Lawrence had finally met his match.

Since Joel had met his match, he decided to stop
worrying about Lawrence for the evening. Besides, he
had to get home to continue the *real* celebration with
his woman.

DON'T MISS
THIS SEXY NEW SERIES
FROM KIMANI ROMANCE!

THE BRADDOCKS

SECRET SON

Power, passion and politics
are all in the family.

HER LOVER'S LEGACY by Adrianne Byrd
August 2008

SEX AND THE SINGLE BRADDOCK
by Robyn Amos
September 2008

SECOND CHANCE, BABY by A.C. Arthur
October 2008

THE OBJECT OF HIS PROTECTION
by Brenda Jackson
November 2008

KIMANI™
ROMANCE

www.kimanipress.com

KPBSS0808

The second title in a passionate new miniseries…

THE BRADDOCKS

SECRET SON

*Power, passion and politics
are all in the family.*

Sex and the Single Braddock

ROBYN AMOS

Determined to uncover the mystery of her powerful father's
death, Shondra Braddock goes to work for Stewart Industries
CEO Connor Stewart. But her undercover mission soon
gets sidetracked when their sizzling attraction explodes
into a secret, jet-setting affair!

Available the first week of September wherever books are sold.

KIMANI™
ROMANCE

www.kimanipress.com

KPRA0810908

All work and no play…

SUITE
Temptation

Acclaimed Author
ANITA
BUNKLEY

When Riana Cole kissed Andre Preaux goodbye to conquer
the San Antonio business world, Andre had given up without
a fight. Now, years later, they are reunited, and memories
of delicious passion come flooding back. Andre is
determined to get her back, but this time he's negotiating
for one thing only—her heart.

"Anita Bunkley's descriptive winter scenery, likable,
well-written characters and engaging story make
Suite Embrace very entertaining."
—*Romantic Times BOOKreviews*

Available the first week of September wherever books are sold.

KIMANI™
ROMANCE

www.kimanipress.com

KPAB0800908

She was on a rescue mission;
he was bent on seduction!

SECRET AGENT
S E D U C T I O N

TOP SECRET
ROMANCE ON THE RUN

Favorite Author

Maureen Smith

Secret Service agent Lia Charles needs all her
professional objectivity to rescue charismatic
revolutionary Armand Magliore, because extracting him
from the treacherous jungle is the easy part—guarding
her heart against the irresistible rebel is the *real* challenge.

Available the first week of September wherever books are sold.

KIMANI
ROMANCE™

www.kimanipress.com KPMS0820908

For All We Know

NATIONAL BESTSELLING AUTHOR
SANDRA KITT

Michaela Landry's quiet summer of
house-sitting takes a dramatic turn when
she finds a runaway teen and brings him
to the nearest hospital. There she meets
Cooper Smith Townsend, a local pastor
whose calm demeanor and dedication are
as attractive as his rugged good looks.
Now their biggest challenge will be to trust
that a passion neither planned for is strong
enough to overcome any obstacle.

Coming the first week of September 2008,
wherever books are sold.

ARABESQUE®

www.kimanipress.com KPSKI040908